Aria has never made decisions for herself—it seems life makes them for her, which is how she's become a star on the hit western TV show REDEMPTION FALLS. Now it seems she's landed herself with a fiancé she doesn't exactly want. No way is she getting hitched, so it's high time she does something about it. But she didn't plan to be a runaway bride—it just sort of happened.

Wheeler is not only laid up with a broken foot but his horse is on watch with a tough injury too. Hobbling to the barn is a trial and his work as a wrangler is off limits. When he goes out to attempt morning chores, he finds a beautiful woman asleep in his barn. Discovering she is a famous actor from the show filming nearby is even less shocking than her plea for him to keep her hidden. Letting her stay on his fixer-upper ranch is an easy yes when she proves she knows how to tend his injured horse, and just looking at her alluring curves does a whole lot for his low spirits.

Aria can't hide forever, but she's reluctant to leave her cozy retreat. The hunky—and stubborn—cowboy provides no pressure as well as a much-needed listening ear. Besides, here on his ranch she finally feels she's doing something she enjoys and making decisions, even if they aren't all for her. After an opportunity falls into Wheeler's lap, she can't let it pass by. But now she isn't sure if she took the leap for him or for herself. What if it ends up benefiting both?

6-Pack Wrangler

by

Em Petrova

Chapter One

A damn fine day. Or it had been before Wheeler's mount had wedged his foot in the V of a branch and gone down in one quick, thousand-pound rush.

Brush was flashing past his eyes, and then he was face down on the ground with the horse half rolled onto his leg. But that wasn't his concern as much as feeling the stirrup around his boot and knowing that his foot was busted.

"Fuck," he ground out, pushing onto his elbows and twisting to look at the horse. The animal lay on its side, and a swift glance at its hoof revealed it was still caught in the branch that had been their demise.

That branch could possibly end the horse's life.

Wheeler reached down to grab his calf. Bracing a hand on each side, he attempted to pull but without engaging the leg muscle and causing more pain to his foot. He tugged with both hands and dug his free foot into the soft earth to scoot away from the horse's body at the same time.

Pain hit him and he grunted, but he'd had worse, like once getting kicked in the thigh so close to his man parts that he'd been sure he'd be singing soprano

1

for the rest of his life. From that, he'd earned a hell of a nasty bruise on his leg, and it'd taken a month to return to the natural color of his skin.

One more shove backward and he should be free. He planted his heel and pushed hard. His backside slid across the ground, and he yanked his leg at the same time. His boot slipped out of the stirrup, but that left it throbbing and already swelling in his boot.

No matter. He had his wits at least, and he had to make sure the horse would survive this fall.

He sure as hell hoped so, because he and Gusto had been a team for the last six years and he'd hate to lose a good mount. With his pain sensors blaring, and Wheeler ignoring them, he shifted to look at the horse. Its eyes were wide and staring with agony, and it was starting to froth a bit around the mouth.

"Easy, boy. Easy now. That's it." He rubbed a hand along its neck and got onto his knees. His foot dragging across the ground made him cuss, and he bit back a yelp of pain. He couldn't frighten the horse more than it already was.

Half afraid to check its leg still caught in the broken limb he hadn't seen before it was too late, he first reached for his shotgun.

He hoped to hell he wouldn't need it. But if it came to that...

Yeah, he'd pull the trigger and end Gusto's suffering. Then he'd probably cry like a baby all the way back to his place and it wouldn't be from his own broken bones.

"Easy," he crooned to the horse and moved to its leg. The swelling was alarming, already alerting him to the severity of the injury.

With a hand on Gusto's side to reassure him, Wheeler slid his fingers along the horse's fetlock. Closing his eyes, he used his sense of touch to root out broken bones. He blew out a breath through his nostrils and moved back up the leg, before sliding down it again and feeling his way.

Thank God, it wasn't broken. But it was bad enough, possibly a torn tendon that could still put the horse out of commission.

Only way to find out was to get him free of the branch and onto his feet.

If Wheeler could get on his own feet first.

Tucking his discomfort into a corner of his mind that he couldn't readily access, he disentangled the branch from Gusto's leg and threw it like a frisbee far into the ravine they rode the edge of. A few more feet in that direction and they would have fallen over the side. Riding was always a bit of a risk in these Washington mountains, and he knew that. Today he was getting a harsh reminder.

"C'mon now, boy. Up." He lurched to his own feet and grabbed the reins. With the toe of his boot barely grazing the ground, he felt all too keenly how bad his foot was. He shoved the sensation away and focused on Gusto, staring down at his leg, which the horse did not gather beneath him in an attempt to get up.

"Let's go, boy. If I can do it, so can you. Up!" He pulled on the reins and slapped him in the flank.

The horse rolled onto its haunches, and Wheeler looked him in the eyes. "We got this, you and me. Up now." One more tug had the horse shoving upward. Wheeler bent to examine its leg in this position, ignoring his own precarious balance. He steadied himself by leaning into Gusto's side and felt along the tendons again. Yeah, swelling like a bee sting to the face, and now Wheeler had to figure out how to get them both safely down the mountain. There wasn't any cell service up here—no use trying.

"Now for the real test," he muttered. No way could he ride the horse in this condition, so that meant he was leading him down on foot. "We're both in for a world of hurt."

He drew Gusto forward, watching his gait to make sure the leg wouldn't buckle. He bore the weight, thank God, but with a pronounced limp that would definitely do more damage to the leg by the time they reached home.

He took hold of the saddle, leaning on it by way of a crutch, and took a limping step of his own.

Fuck, that hurt. Good thing his boot was tight—it held together the bones almost like a splint. Didn't mean it felt good, though.

After a dozen steps between them, Wheeler realized it might be nightfall before he reached the ranch and got medical attention for either. Unless by some crazy miracle the mountain allowed cell signals to pass and he could make a call to his buddy King. But he wouldn't hold his breath.

Or he would, as he took the next step and the next. After a mile, he was getting into a groove. Hobble, lean on horse, grit teeth against pain. Repeat. Gusto seemed to be holding up better but horses were like that — tough to the end. Wheeler's eyes burned with a tear of appreciation for his horse, and then he blinked it away.

He paused to let the animal drink from a mountain stream, and he took a swig from his thermos in the saddle bag. Too bad he didn't have any wrap for the horse's leg. Although, he did have a blanket and some jerky. If he needed to, they could sleep rough on the mountain.

No, they could make it to his ranch. The small outdated house that had been his grandparents' had never sounded so inviting.

All the way across uneven ground, he feared he'd fall and break something else, or Gusto would go down and not get up again, and he would need to resort to the shotgun. But that didn't happen.

When the glimmer of moonlight shone on the new metal roof of the house, Wheeler felt like letting out a cheer. If he had any steam left in him, he would.

He got the horse to the barn and knelt to tend its foot. Wrapping it tight enough to support, but not so tight it cut off blood supply, was all he could manage right now, and he still needed to make it to the house without the horse for support in order to make a call from the landline.

Being remote seems like a good idea until you get into trouble.

Navigating the saggy porch steps gave him the resolve to rebuild them the minute he was able, and by the time he reached the kitchen and the phone, he was panting with exertion and a fair amount of pain.

He punched King's number. It was suppertime and his friend might be in the middle of dinner with his pretty little wife, but this moment was what made King a good friend.

"King," he said the moment he picked up.

"What's wrong? Your voice sounds rough."

"I got trouble. I need the vet for Gusto. He's in the barn. And a ride for myself to the ER."

"Shit. Be there in a few. Sit tight, man."

"If I sit down, you'll have to throw me over your shoulder to get me to the truck. I'll be in the barn with the horse."

* * * * *

Aria went to her closet and pulled some of her favorite tops off hangers. With these slung over her arm, she headed back to the bed and her open suitcase. She folded each top meticulously and placed it in the bottom and then circled back to her closet.

"Why don't you leave the packing to your assistant?" Jason's voice came at her in the depths of her closet.

"How would she know what I want to wear during times I'm not in wardrobe?" she called back.

For a week since Jason had learned she was heading to Washington and the set of *Redemption Falls*, he'd been in a funk. Pouting like a little boy who wasn't getting his way. Well, he'd have to get over it. He was an actor too and as professionals, they did their jobs without complaint. And there would be no complaint from her anyway—she was headed to the mountains. For a Montana rancher's daughter, she couldn't be happier to return to something more familiar than streets lined with designer clothing shops and A-list parties.

She came out carrying several pairs of her jeans, some leggings and her favorite feminine tuxedo she had worn to one of the last awards shows. There, Bellarose Abbott had won big time for her role on *Redemption Falls* and some said this was Aria's year, but since she was only a side character, playing the cousin of Bellarose's character, she didn't think so.

Dumping all the garments on the bed, she slanted a look at Jason, who perched on the edge. In jeans and a white T-shirt, with the perfect scruff of five o'clock shadow, he was as hunky as they came. Women flocked to Jason Lee wherever they went, and it wasn't because he was an action hero. His boy-next-door looks had every female — and plenty of males too — drooling over him.

"Aria. You'll be gone for months. How will we keep this alive?"

She pressed her lips together. "Other people do. We have to learn to work with our careers and relationships."

"Why don't you sound concerned about it?" He caught her wrist mid-fold, and she looked up into his eyes. Blue eyes that had melted her panties off at the start. But now…

Well, the distance would do them good. At least in her mind. It would give her time to figure things out.

Like how she had gotten herself a live-in boyfriend in the first place, when she hadn't asked for one. He'd just sort of shown up with a bag and hadn't left. That had been four months ago.

She let him reel her closer. His expensive aftershave hit her nose, and she let out a sigh. He moved her to stand between his legs and placed his hands on her hips.

"I'm going to miss you so much." His gritty voice was something he was known for and used in every action movie to hook the women into paying good money to see him.

"I'll miss you too." She said it automatically, but did she feel it? Yes, she definitely needed that distance.

He pulled her closer, staring into her eyes. "We'll Facetime every day."

"Of course."

"And text each other whenever you aren't on set." It was too bad that Jason was between jobs at the moment. Otherwise, his time would be consumed and this wouldn't be an issue. Who knew the tough guy he was known for being was so damn clingy in real life?

"Yes, we'll text." She patted his shoulder in reassurance.

"Then when you come back, you can start planning the wedding."

She froze, eyes wide and her heart making no sound at all.

It must have stopped.

Great, he'd killed her with a marriage proposal.

Wait—*a what?*

She unfroze her eyelids and managed to blink at him. "A… wedding?" Her voice came out faint, and she felt she might do just that, with her head spinning like this.

"Yes!" He grabbed her up and tossed her down on the bed, hovering over her with stars in his eyes.

Oh God. How do I get myself into these situations?

She hadn't set out to be an actor—she'd begun on the other end of the camera, handling the horses on set. Then at one point she'd been a body double and bam! A role was written into the show for her and now she was on the other side of the camera, when all she had wanted to do was work with horses.

But how could she turn down an opportunity that millions of people would jump at?

Months later, her assistant told her Jason Lee had called, and Aria's response had been, "That's nice." And when she'd been informed he was taking her out for dinner tonight at the elite new club in Hollywood, what was she to say?

Then the moving in… sharing a bed and a closet. Ugh. Now a wedding?

She didn't know what to say—her vocal cords had taken a nap. Or were in a coma.

"The minute you get back to California, you can get started with the plans. I have some time and can be checking out venues. I'll send you some pics and video so you get a good idea before you even begin."

Lord help me.

She just stared up at Jason, which he mistook for shock. Well, it was after a fashion.

He chuckled. "Why do you look so stunned, sweetheart? You know you mean the world to me. I love you and you love me. Why not make it official and while we're apart, you'll have something to look forward to."

"It's just that..." She raised a hand to his shoulder. "I'm not entirely sure I *want* to plan a wedding."

"Then we'll hire someone." He leaned in and kissed her hard.

With the discussion ended, she managed to finish packing even while in a daze.

Now she sat on a plane, staring out at the blanket of clouds. Far below was a world where people knew what they wanted and how to get it. She knew what *she* wanted, but then something else came along and she sort of went along with it.

This was Aria's biggest fault, and one that she needed to get therapy for as soon as possible or be forever tied to an actor she didn't love.

"Can I get you anything, Miss Bloom?"

She looked up at the flight attendant in first class. "Um, some Evian please." On second thought... "And a scotch and soda."

"Of course. Are you comfortable? Would you like a hot towel?"

"Not right now, thank you." She offered a smile, and the woman returned it before moving off to the next person.

Aria stared out the window and wondered what her daddy would say when he read the headline about her engagement, which Jason would surely spill to the media and Aria hadn't exactly agreed to. Crap, how was she ever going to explain this to anybody? The people on set would want to hear details, she'd have interviews, Jason would be texting photos of venues…

She wanted to throw up.

How had a Montana girl with countrified dreams of competing in national horse competitions even become an actor and now have a famous fiancé?

She was just about to drop her face into her hands to stifle a wail, but the attendant returned with her scotch and soda. She took it with a polite smile but dropped the mask the moment she wasn't the center of attention anymore. She brought the drink to her lips.

Well, she could commit herself to day drinking even if she couldn't commit to marriage.

Chapter Two

Aria stood at the edge of the field, the wind ruffling like fingers through her loose brown hair as she stared off at the mountains. Yes, it was home.

Funny thing was, she was meant to be acting a scene. The cameras were rolling, the producer was staring at her intensely to make sure she gave the performance he wanted from her. But she'd just been beaten over the head with the realization that it was the mountains that felt like home, not the state and when a tear zigzagged down her cheek, it was real as hell.

She was crying for the beauty of it all and grateful for the sanctuary Washington was offering her from the hell that hadn't yet broken loose around her.

How was it possible Jason hadn't said a word? The story of their engagement wasn't out. She had spent two weeks now perching on horseshoe nails, just waiting for the world to blow up in her face.

She wrapped an arm around the fence post and slowly lowered her head to rest against the rough wood.

"Good! And cut!"

The producer's call filled her ears, but Aria didn't immediately move away from the fence post. She felt like tethering herself to it and becoming part of the beauty of the Washington ranch they were filming on.

Dickson, her producer, was coming toward her. She straightened to give him a smile, wiping away what was supposed to be a fake tear.

"That was heart-wrenching and lovely at the same time. Well done, Aria. Every day I work with you I'm shocked anew at your natural talent for acting."

She was pretty sure if given any role besides a rancher's niece that she would suck at it.

"Thank you," she said.

Dickson peered out from under his own cowboy hat. He was one of the many rich industry people who owned ranches, and his happened to be right here in Washington. He had promised to throw a party there soon so she would get to see it.

"Are you all right?" he asked.

She gave a small laugh. "Of course I am."

"I wondered for a moment when you kept holding on to that fence."

"Just homesick, I guess."

"This has to be the next best thing to being home, isn't it?" He was like a favorite uncle to her, supportive yet tough if you made a misstep, and she liked him all the better for it.

She nodded. "It's beautiful and I'm so glad to work here."

"Good. Then I'm glad. Now why don't you go get into makeup for the next scene?"

With a nod, she strode off toward the big event tent that was serving as their makeup and wardrobe changing station. When she walked in, several pairs of eyes watched her.

Feeling self-conscious, she lifted a hand to pull off her cowgirl hat. By the time she made it to her makeup chair, everybody was staring outright.

Her assistant's grin really set her off, though.

"What is going on?" she asked.

At that moment, music sounded through some speakers, filling the tent. She hopped off the seat and looked around. A wedding march. What the hell was going on?

She spun in a circle and near the back of the tent saw a flurry of motion. Then Jason Lee stepped out of a knot of people. He was dressed in a tuxedo with his hair rumpled like he'd just dashed his fingers through it. He was grinning in that bad-boy way that scorched every camera that turned his way.

And he was coming for her.

A step behind him was one of the assistants carrying a sleek white gown of satin and even from here, Aria could see the train.

Panic hit her square in the chest. She couldn't draw breath, her feet cemented to the floor.

Oh God, he was coming and there was no escape.

As Jason reached her and took her by the hands, he dropped into a debonair pose on one knee and drew a ring from his pocket. He pinched the platinum and diamond between thumb and forefinger and stared up into her eyes.

"Aria Bloom, will you do me the honor of being my wife?"

She didn't have any air to gasp. Nor did she have a single word floating around her head to shoot out onto her tongue. *C'mon, Aria, all you need is a little NO.*

But she was blank. Hell, a newborn babe had more thoughts rolling around its head than she did at the moment.

His gaze penetrated her, and she felt everyone closing in. The sensation of being squeezed intensified. She took a breath, but it was choppy and her heart erratic.

"I know I don't deserve you, but I promise to love you the rest of our days." Jason added, giving her the impression he was trying to fill the awkward silence.

A collective sigh sounded in the tent as every single person was touched by the romantic sentiment. Every person except the bride.

This couldn't be happening.

It was.

She had to make some decision—she'd scolded herself for this very thing during her entire flight to

Washington. Take charge, speak up for herself. Don't let life bowl her over.

Jason drew her hand closer and slipped the ring into place.

Her heart gave a hard jerk in her chest as applause sounded. Jason swept to his feet, gathered her up and bent her over his arm to kiss her. When he pulled her upright again, she stared at him in shock.

"Since you seemed worried about all the details of the wedding, I brought the wedding to you. Here is your dress, chosen by your favorite LA stylist. She says it will fit you like a glove and you will be glowing in it. Which we all know already."

Everyone laughed.

She was in a nightmare. Or a circus tent with her in the center ring while clowns and animals performed around her—life moving while she stood frozen.

"Jason—"

He traced a thumb down the curve of her cheek. "Put on your wedding gown and I will see you at the altar."

"The altar?"

"Yes, the set crew worked so hard to do this for you both!" Her assistant bounced on her toes. She took Aria by the arm and led her away from Jason, who continued to stare at her and she back at him, though for very different reasons.

The other assistant ran along beside them carrying the dress. Aria ended up in her trailer and damn if she wasn't surrounded by gorgeous roses. Dozens and dozens overflowing the space, as if she wasn't claustrophobic enough.

When the assistant hung the gown on a hook and she was truly forced to look at it, a sob wrenched her.

"Oh, Aria. You deserve this surprise wedding! I'm so happy for you!" her assistant said.

No. No, no, no. "No." She said the last aloud.

Take charge. Take what you want, and it is not this.

She shook her head. Tears were streaming down her cheeks, but she couldn't compose herself if she tried. A cry left her, and she tore the ring off her finger and thrust it at her assistant.

"Take this. Take it all back to him. I can't. Tell him I'm sorry."

She twisted and bolted for the door, shoving it open and running into the field as fast as her feet would carry her. The wind rushed over her, and she didn't slow. Night was falling but there was no way she could go back there, knowing a candlelit ceremony awaited her to marry a man she didn't love and didn't wish to be joined with.

It probably made her an awful person, leaving the way she had, but he'd left her no choice. She felt like a cornered cat, and nobody had respected that her back was up and she was hissing—they'd just corralled her into her trailer and tried to force her into a dress.

Even the dress was all wrong. She never would have chosen that silhouette for a wedding gown. Ever since she was a little girl she'd envisioned herself on horseback on her wedding day, a ball gown enveloping the saddle as she rode down the aisle with her father on a mount beside her to give her away.

No, this felt wrong down to the toes of her boots.

She ran on.

After she reached a dirt road, she slowed her pace, certain nobody would find her here. By now, someone must have sent a car to search for her, and she didn't want to be found. She needed time.

She walked for another mile up the dirt road, wondering if it was really a fire access for the mountain. Just when she was beginning to think she would end up deep in the mountains alone and should turn back, she caught a glimmer of light ahead.

A truck? She moved her neck, trying to see through the thick trees. Another hundred yards of walking and she made out the house, the outlines small but sturdy, and a warm yellow light projected through the front windows.

But she wasn't about to walk up to a house and say she'd just run away from her wedding.

Her feet continued to carry her forward anyway. She had nowhere else to go, and she was pulled along by instinct. When she spotted the barn off to the left, she realized why.

Drawn to a structure she knew and loved most, she walked up to the side door and put her hand on the splintery old wood. At first she wondered if there were animals even kept here, and then she heard a shifting sound of hooves on straw.

She pushed open the door and went inside.

* * * * *

Wheeler reached for the crutches, which were somehow always just out of reach. And here, his entire life, he'd prided himself on his long arms.

He balanced on one foot and leaned to the side. Getting out of the shower — and *taking* one — was the hardest part. The crutches were just another agitation to add to his growing list over the past few days since breaking his foot.

He growled with frustration and made a lunge for the crutches, putting his casted foot down despite doctor's orders not to bear weight on it. He shoved the crutches beneath his arms and stumped his way — buck naked — to his bedroom.

Of course his Wranglers didn't fit over his cast, so he'd resorted to wearing sweats, which wasn't at all cowboy-like. He perched on the edge of his bed to slide on his boxers and the sweats. Then he grabbed the first shirt he saw, which happened to be a western denim one with pearl buttons.

Putting on one sock and cowboy boot felt wrong as hell, and by the time he finished, he was beginning to question how many more mornings like this he could live through. The doc said six weeks with a possibility of eight.

Two whole months of not being of any use to King up on his ranch, Blackwater, or hell, even managing to care for his own three measly horses burned his ass. Wheeler set his molars together and clomped into the kitchen.

The noise of his crutches on the old worn tile floors irritated him so much that he groaned. When he made it to the kitchen, he abandoned one crutch by leaning it against the cabinet and balanced on the other while he fixed himself some eggs.

He cracked them into the pan with a pat of butter. Usually he ate his eggs over easy, but today he was in such a funk that he ran the spatula through them, breaking the yolks and semi-scrambling all of it.

By the time he sat at the small table for two that his grandparents had taken their coffee at every morning of their retirement years, Wheeler forked up his eggs and swallowed without relish.

Everything was goddamn bleak. There—he'd said it. It might just be a foot, and Lord knew people out there had much worse to contend with, but he was ticked to be out of commission. Luckily, he lived on little wages and had enough saved up to get him by without working for King. Though his friend had offered to continue his wages, Wheeler couldn't allow him to do that.

He dumped his plate and fork in the sink with the other growing pile of dirty dishes there and then settled his hat on his head. For the past few days since he'd broken his foot, King and the other ranch hand who helped him out, Schmitty, had been coming to tend Wheeler's horses.

The vet had come and gone a time or two as well, checking on Gusto's leg. A suspensory ligament tear that would take much longer than Wheeler's foot to heal.

If it heals at all.

The possibility was still there. Wrapping the leg and keeping the horse on rest was the course for now, but too much rest and he'd get stiff. Wheeler felt his pain. After days of doing so little, he'd rolled out of bed a little stiffer than usual too. And he was damn sick of these crutches digging in under his arms.

Outside, he cursed the dilapidated state of his front porch steps once again and made his way painstakingly down them. Navigating the uneven ground with a gimp foot was no better and a huge test of his patience. Every step had to be calculated first and then executed precisely or he'd end up on his ass again, this time with a broken leg or arm.

He fixed his stare on the barn and set his resolve. At least it was decent weather and he wasn't doing this in a Washington downpour, which typically came with a stiff mountain wind.

By the time he reached the barn, he heard the horses inside shifting with eagerness to get some attention. He'd texted King that he was going to try to do the chores himself and his buddy had told him to text back if he couldn't manage. But he knew Wheeler would — they were cut from the same cloth.

When he pushed open the door, one of his pair of mares let out a nicker of greeting. "Hello to you too," he crooned. He left the door open behind him to allow in more light. The barn needed some updates but that would come in good time. For now, it served the purpose and he'd only inherited the property two years before.

He planted the crutches onto the dusty floor and swung himself forward.

He froze midway and nearly dumped himself on the floor. Scrambling to right himself, he stared at the far stall that no horse occupied. And it was a good thing too, because a woman slept there, curled in the straw.

His heart gave a hard lurch, and he shoved forward. Was she alive? Had some drug junkie picked his barn to overdose in?

Reaching the stall door, he braced a hand on the wood and gazed down at the figure. She lay on her side, face tipped toward the soft straw he replaced in the corner when he did the other stalls, though he rarely placed a horse here.

She wore jeans — ones with holes put there by a manufacturer and not hard work. Her plaid top was twisted on her body from rolling and the barest glimpse of tan skin, like coffee with a lot of milk,

23

peeked out between her top and the waist of her jeans. As he skimmed his eyes up over her curves — hip, waist, breasts — he spent some time studying her hair, tangled and tumbling over her shoulder.

He stared at her chest for a long moment, watching for a rise and fall. When he spotted it, a breath he'd been holding trickled out. She was alive. But for how long?

Using the crutch, he tapped it against the sole of her cowgirl boot. No movement. He did it again, and this time, she rolled onto her back, her face now visible through the webbed strands of her rich brown hair.

Damn, she had to have delicate features and a full mouth, didn't she? Suddenly, he felt bad about waking her.

He tapped her again on the boot, and she woke with a wild jerk. Bolting into a sitting position, eyes wild from behind her hair dangling over them. Not bothering to move her hair from her vision, she leaped to her feet.

"Who are you?" she cried out.

The woman had balls, he'd give her that. Demanding answers from him when she was the one camping in his barn?

"Who are *you*?" he returned.

"Are you the owner?"

He gave a single nod. Their gazes connected, and he noted how fast she was breathing.

"I'm so sorry. I meant to leave by morning."

"It's just dawn. I came down early to see to the horses."

She dropped her stare over his crutches to the fat cast on his foot. His toes were bare, because he'd forgotten to cover them with the stupid sock thing.

"How'd you break your foot?"

"How'd you end up sleeping in my barn? You'd better start giving me some answers, woman."

She hugged herself and eyed him. "I needed a place to stay."

"Where ya from? I've never seen you in these parts, and it might be big country but we all know each other."

"Passing through."

He didn't believe it for a minute but went along with it. "Where from?"

"Montana."

He'd been watching her eyes when she replied and there wasn't even a glimmer there that revealed she was lying to him. Good—Wheeler hated a liar. The last person to lie to him had been promptly evicted from his life, and he hadn't dated since.

"All right, Montana. What are ya running from?"

Her eyes widened just a tiny bit, but it was enough for him to notice. Especially since he was having a difficult time looking away from the true beauty of those eyes, brown and fringed heavily with

25

black lashes. Looking closer, he saw a streak of makeup smudged across the crest of her cheek, like she'd cried off what makeup she was wearing.

"I told you, I'm just passing through. I'm sorry for sleeping in your barn and I'll be on my way now." She didn't move, though, and he wasn't convinced it was because he blocked the stall. She didn't seem eager to leave.

"Are you high?"

"What?" Her voice rose a pitch. "Are you serious?"

"Yeah."

"Of course I'm not high! I've never touched drugs in my life!"

"And you haven't been drinking. I'd smell it on you."

"Aren't you observant." Sarcasm dripped from the whispered words.

Somehow, he liked her more for it. He'd probably smile if he didn't feel so damn angry at the world right now.

That made him remember the horse, and he turned away from the stall toward Gusto. The gelding nudged the door to be let out. King or Schmitty had been letting him out to graze and coming back to tuck him in at night. Wheeler would do the same, though first he needed to check his wrapping. If he saw any increase in the swelling of that leg, he'd need to take action and fast.

It was damn awkward to use the crutches in the barn but more so to open the door and balance on one foot while trying to tend the horse. The mares on either side of Gusto let Wheeler know they were displeased to be kept waiting.

"You gotta be patient with me, girls. I'm lame and it will take a bit, but I promise to get to ya."

A boot heel scraped on the floor behind him. "Can I help?"

"Nah, I got it." She might be dressed like a country girl but that didn't make her one. Probably some city girl running away from a controlling daddy or boyfriend. Wheeler couldn't guess her age, but he'd put her below twenty-five.

He patted Gusto and soothed him for a moment before tentatively moving into a crouch to see that front leg. It was wrapped in cotton batting and standing wraps, the ends overlapping to stabilize it. Gusto let Wheeler have the leg and tolerated having the wraps removed, then the tendon palpated even though it was painful.

"I know that hurts, boy. Easy. Just checking for swelling."

"Tendon injury?" the woman asked from behind.

Wheeler checked his surprise. "Yeah, happened a few days ago."

"A fall?"

"Yeah."

"And that's how you broke your foot too."

He tossed her a look over his shoulder. "That's right."

One of the mares hit the stall door to be let out, and Wheeler released Gusto's hoof. He set it back down gently and awkwardly rewrapped the lower leg. Satisfied he'd done it right, Wheeler unhooked a rope from a nail outside the stall and used it as a lead. When he reached the doors to let the horse loose into the fenced area, he struggled with the crutches, the latch and the horse.

The woman moved forward quickly. "Let me help." She flicked the latch like she did this every day of her life and pushed the doors open. Wheeler loosened the rope and let the horse go free. Gusto took some odd steps into the pasture.

"Probably stiff," she said quietly as if musing it to herself.

Wheeler looked at her. With her wild hair and wrinkled clothes, she might be down and out, but her voice and the way she held herself spoke of breeding.

"Who are you again?" he asked.

"Aria."

"Aria," he repeated.

Her face turned three shades of red before settling on the darkest hue. "Yeah, just Aria."

"Okay then. I'm Wheeler."

"Can I help with the mares?"

"I'm afraid if I say no, they're going to knock down their doors." By now both mares were angry with him and showing it. The wood of the stalls cracked and shuddered with their sharp movements.

"Sassy ones, aren't they? Sisters?" Aria went to one stall and opened it. He noted how she stood back as she did so, in case the horse rushed forward. Seemed like she knew some about livestock.

She's beautiful too.

His awareness of her was new to him—hell, he hadn't felt even a twinge at a woman's nearness in a long time. Even a beautiful mess, Aria intrigued him.

She was looking at him, waiting for his answer to her question.

"Yeah, they're sisters, foals from different years but they get along well enough and they preen over Gusto."

"Is that the injured gelding?"

"Yeah." He made a move to reach for the mare he was tending and his crutch fell to the floor. He grunted.

"Let me get it."

"I got it." Before she could help, he bent and snatched it up, dragging the wooden device across the floor until he could draw it up under his arm again. "Damn things."

"I've never been on crutches myself, but I've had relatives on them, and they were grumpy as old bears the entire time." She slanted a look his way.

"You calling me grumpy?"

29

"I don't know your usual personality, but you seem a bit crabby."

He huffed air through his nostrils. Again, her words didn't annoy him as much as... intrigue him? It had been too long since he'd had a woman, if that was the case. After all, a woman with a mouth on her wasn't exactly foreplay. Or was it?

While she dealt with one mare, he watched to ensure she knew what she was doing. She was gentle, he'd give her that, talking low to the horse who was unfamiliar with her and slowly winning her over so Aria was allowed to stroke her neck.

Aria laughed. The soft tinkling sound gathered up Wheeler's raw nerves and tugged. What the hell was that about? He wasn't himself since breaking his foot. That must be it.

"You're just begging for attention, aren't ya, girl?" For the first time, he saw Aria smile.

The moment seemed to stand still, stretch out and linger like the warmth of the sun long after the moon rose.

"Yes, you're a good girl." She patted the mare's nose. "What's her name?"

"She's called Maisy but I like to think of her as Runs for the Hills."

"Why is that?" Aria didn't look away from the horse, obviously smitten with the animal's reaction to being stroked.

"The minute she gets loose, she makes a break for it. Found her halfway up that mountain two different times. Not something I want to do again, especially for the next two months."

She nodded and expertly secured the halter with the lead rope to take her outside. He did the same, though much more slowly, inching along on the crutches. Once all three animals were secured inside the fence, Wheeler closed the barn doors again.

Aria looked around. "Do they get supplement feeds?"

"The grazing's enough for now. Later, I'll give them a little something."

"All right." She looked nervous, eyes downcast. No wonder, because they were two strangers who'd just performed a chore that Wheeler thought of as intimate. Anything to do with stock was sacred and almost ritual. He'd felt it before with guys he worked with—ranchers, other hands and wranglers alike. Camaraderie formed quickly. He'd just never expected to feel it with this woman who'd been sleeping in his barn.

"Has…" She stopped abruptly and gave him a desperate look.

Waiting, he arched a brow.

"Has anyone been here looking for me?"

"No."

She seemed to melt in front of his eyes, shoulders slumping forward and relief passing across her pretty features. "Thank God. Can you just... not say anything about finding me here?"

He lifted both brows now. "Depends."

"On?"

"If you're running from the law."

"Not the law — a boyfriend. Or fiancé. A wedding. Oh God."

Wheeler watched her grow more agitated and upset with each stuttering word that fell from her lips. And it was as he'd guessed from the start — a man was involved. While he didn't want some dude showing up here looking for his fiancé, Wheeler couldn't exactly ignore her plea for help.

"Why don't you come up to the house, have some coffee."

She looked up at him, her lips parting slightly, with a trace of disbelief in her eyes. After a few heartbeats, she gave a nod.

He went out of the barn, and she followed alongside him, though she could walk much faster. It was hard not to ask about the fiancé/wedding thing, but he could pretty much gather the information just from those two words. Some man was trying to corner her into marrying him and she'd run scared.

Wheeler found he didn't like that.

"Watch your step here. The wood needs replaced."

"It's you who should be watching your step."

"Tell me about it. Damn things." He set the crutches onto the second step up and pushed onto the first, swinging his casted foot as he slowly made his way up.

Inside the house, she paused to look around. He wondered what she was seeing. To him, it was home. Some things still remained from the years his grandparents had lived here, but he'd replaced some of the items that weren't him, like knickknacks or the pair of ugly lamps he'd hated growing up.

"It's not much," he heard himself say. What did he care what she thought of his home?

"Just needs some sprucing up." Direct, was what he'd call her.

He snorted. "You're not wrong. It was my grandparents' place before they passed away. I've done little to it since."

"You won't be anytime soon, either. You can barely manage the horses, what few you have."

Okay, this was bordering on judgmental and he wasn't abiding that. Who was she to comment on his lifestyle at all?

"I don't earn a living off the ranch. Just keep the horses for the love of it. I got plenty of outdoor work elsewhere. Let's get that coffee." With an abrupt statement like that, he hoped she took the hint and kept the comments to herself. She followed him to the kitchen and watched him fumble with crutches, mugs and coffee.

"I hope you don't take sugar, because I'm out."

"No. Cream?" She made a move to the fridge, and he nodded that she should go ahead and grab it for herself.

"Grab a couple eggs while you're at it."

"Are you hungry?" she asked, turning from the fridge with the jug of milk.

"No, but you must be. Eggs are my specialty."

"I couldn't ask you to make me breakfast."

"I'm offering and I can manage fine. Sit and have your coffee. You must have had a rough night in the barn and could use the caffeine."

"What I'd like is a toothbrush."

He looked at her. "Got an extra in the bathroom drawer. Uh… through that doorway and first door on your right." He gestured with his crutch.

She stood, coffee forgotten. "Thank you, Wheeler."

As she left the room, he watched her go, all round ass in fitted denim and long hair swaying on her spine. Damn if he wasn't finding himself strangely connected to her. Either it was his natural urge to protect that made him strive to put her at ease, or he was just bored senseless being laid up this way and needed the diversion.

With those curves of hers, it could be coming from the surge of testosterone in my system.

* * * * *

Wheeler's bathroom was straight out of the 1980s, complete with a baby blue sink and bathtub. His mention that it had been his grandparents' home made her envision floral accents and perhaps a goose or two holding tiny soaps. But he had only the basics — toilet paper stacked on the back of the toilet, a razor and shaving cream on the sink — which was such a guy thing.

She closed the door behind herself and found the geese she'd expected — on a strip of wallpaper border he hadn't ripped off all the way. She stood there for a long moment, collecting herself.

She'd really messed up, hadn't she? She'd run from the impromptu wedding — what woman wanted that, anyway? — and from Jason Lee, a man who would not take being jilted lightly. Rumors were sure to fly about her just to save his reputation.

Clapping a hand to her mouth, she realized if she was discovered here at this small ranch with a cowboy, the rumors would fall into his lap too. Wheeler was innocent and didn't deserve the viciousness of the media if she was found out.

But who would know to look here? It was the reason she'd chosen it, after all.

With a glance at her reflection, she saw hollows beneath her eyes that would make her makeup girl *tsk* in displeasure. But the rest of her...

God, when was the last time she'd seen such life in her eyes or pink in her cheeks that hadn't been put there by a makeup brush?

It was being back on a ranch—a real one and not just the set of *Redemption Falls*. Even simply touching a horse for her own pleasure and not because it was written into a script felt amazing.

She washed her hands and splashed her face with water. Then she used a fresh towel from a small stack. Wheeler was surprisingly tidy for a single guy, which she guessed he was or a girlfriend would be here fussing over her injured man. It seemed he was not only on his own but isolated. If he went down on those crutches, who would find him?

After locating the toothbrush in the package, she brushed her teeth and felt a thousand times better for it. That was good, because she had something to do and it would take more than a clean mouth to fortify her.

She took out her cell phone. Lucky she'd had it on her when she'd run. Then again, after what she'd done, it could serve as a torment.

When she brought up an app to search the internet, it said not connected. She checked her bars of service and sure enough, there weren't any. Quickly, she tapped a few keys to see if Wheeler might have Wi-Fi.

Of course he didn't.

Crap, now she couldn't check the news about herself, but maybe that was a good thing.

It meant she could possibly hide longer. Just a few more days until she figured out what to say to Jason.

She put away her phone and then went into the kitchen once more. Wheeler's back was to her, broad-shouldered and chiseled from there down. His attire of western shirt and sweatpants made her want to giggle, but she supposed a cowboy couldn't wiggle into a tight pair of jeans with his foot in a cast.

At her footstep, he half turned. "Feel better?"

She nodded, pushing her hair behind her ear. His gaze tracked her action, and it suddenly hit her that she was alone with a man she didn't know. The Hollywood version of herself would never let that happen, but the minute she'd fled from the set, she'd reverted to the Montana rancher's daughter who sized up a man just by the way he treated his stock.

She didn't find herself uncomfortable around the cowboy she didn't know, because he'd been good to his horses, and that just added to the feeling of homecoming.

While he finished frying the eggs and flipped them onto a plate straight from the pan, she crossed the kitchen with the dated white tile floor to take her plate from him. "Thank you."

Their fingers brushed on the edge of the plate, and he pulled back. "Welcome. It's not much, but I'm a little low on supplies. Why don't you sit and eat before it gets cold?"

She did, returning to her coffee too, which was still hot and strong, the way she liked it. He watched her a moment before edging over on his crutches to sit with his leg sticking out to the side.

"Why don't you tell me what happened to your foot and the horse's leg." She forked up some eggs. He watched her take the bite and move it around in her mouth.

"What is it?" he asked.

"Salt?"

"By the stove. I didn't add it because I didn't know if you liked it on eggs."

She got up and fetched it herself, sprinkling her eggs liberally. When she took the next bite, she smiled. "That's just right, buttery and salty."

"A girl who likes country food."

She nodded. "Told ya I'm from Montana. My momma didn't raise a gluten-free kale-loving girl."

That made him smile, and damn if her heart didn't give a mini flip at how damn sexy a smile was on him. From beneath her lashes and under guise of taking another bite, she studied him. Skin tanned from the sun with small creases bordering each hazel eye, a nose that looked to have been broken a time or two... and that mouth. Who knew a crooked smile could make a girl's heart tumble like that?

"Took a bad spill up on the ridge. Knew I'd broken my foot straight off but wasn't so sure about the horse. For a minute, I thought I'd have to put him down."

She winced. To a horse lover, that was the worst possible thing to happen in a lifetime of caring for animals. She'd seen her daddy cry like a baby after putting down one of his favorite horses.

"Good you didn't need to. But you couldn't have ridden him home."

"No. Walked, both of us limping along like a pair of old men. Got home after dark and the vet came right up. Said he's not able to make a call on how it'll heal until the swelling goes down. In a few more days, he can better treat it and give a prognosis."

"Might take several months to a year."

"Yeah." He didn't sound too happy about that, but who would be?

"At least he's not my working horse. He's for pleasure and a few other things I need him for around the place."

"And the mares?" She raised a brow.

He tipped his head. "Why, they're just to keep Gusto company. What man doesn't want a coupla women to fuss over him?"

She couldn't help but smile in response, but she noticed how his eyes dropped to her lips, and again her heart gave a flicker that said, *Oh, hello.*

After she finished eating, she took her plate to the sink. It was piled with other dirty pots and pans and plates, and she started running the water with a squeeze of dish soap.

"You don't gotta do that."

"It's the least I can do for my bed and breakfast."

He snorted. "Not much of either."

"I'd like to do the dishes in repayment." She waited for him to say no, but what bachelor would ever turn down an offer like that? She bit back a smile and turned to the sink again. He got up to fetch another cup of coffee. It took all she could to not take over and carry it back to the table for him, but she recognized a frustrated man when she saw one. An independent one too. The frown between his brows wasn't masking how much he hated his current state of immobility, which was affecting everything from ranch chores to having coffee.

When he settled again, she felt his stare on her back. Until now, she hadn't thought about him not recognizing her. Or maybe he did and just hadn't said so. Well, she wasn't about to bring it up—being famous wasn't something she'd likely ever grow accustomed to.

"So what are your plans now?" His question jerked her from her thoughts.

She swirled the dishcloth over the greasy pan. By the looks of it, he'd been eating a lot of eggs. Or nothing but eggs.

"What do you mean?" She tossed a look over her shoulder.

"While I like not having to be on this foot washing my own dishes, you surely have some idea of what you're doing next."

She let out a breath and turned to face him. "Is it crazy that I don't?"

He stared at her like it was.

Okay, maybe it was. But for once, her life felt like her own, even in this precarious state of indecision. She'd spent too much time letting others make her choices and saying nothing so as not to offend or seem ungrateful for an opportunity.

Right now, she'd decided to wash these dishes.

"Maybe I can take a look at the horse again. Seems like the leg could be iced and rewrapped."

He eyed her, head cocked and his hat pulled lower than before. "You know what you're doing?"

"Seen it done on TV." When his brows shot up, she chuckled. "I'm joking. Yes, I know what I'm doing. The vet told you it needs iced several times a day, didn't he?"

Wheeler nodded. "Been hell doing it on my own."

She sensed she could be intruding on his privacy and might have outworn her welcome. "Look, I'll ice the leg, rewrap it and then be on my way."

"Your way where?"

She shrugged. "Washington seems like a big place. I'm sure I'll figure out something."

When she finished washing the dishes, she dried her hands and neatly draped the towel over the edge of the sink. "You have an ice boot for the horse?"

He laughed. "I've got one horse and never had the funds to spend on a fancy ice boot."

"Oh. Then an old inner tube would work. Fill it with ice and conform it to the swollen area."

He blinked at her.

"Ice pack and wrap?"

"In the freezer. Wrap's down at the barn."

"How high is the injury? Is this something we could use an ice bucket for?" She reached into the freezer, past frozen burger patties and steaks. Not a bag of vegetables in sight. She located an ice pack and pulled it out.

"Ice bucket could work, if you could get Gusto to stand in it. My guess is he might put up a fight. How do you know so much about horses?"

"Told ya—I've seen it on TV."

He started to get up, but she waved him back down. "You should prop up that foot. Your toes look plenty swollen too. I'll handle Gusto." She flashed a grin and headed out the front door, letting the screen slam behind her.

With each step she took toward the barn, she felt lighter, happier than she had in too long. A light bounce hit her heels and by the time she reached the fence she was whistling. Getting Gusto to grow accustomed to her took some time, but soon she had him nosing her hand for more pets.

She was just getting down to business when she heard the screen door bang again.

He just can't sit still.

Wheeler came across the uneven ground, and she kept an eye on him in case he went down. When he made it to the fence, she had the wrap halfway off Gusto's leg.

"How's it look?" Wheeler leaned against the fence.

"Swollen. Your vet doesn't have ultrasound, does he?"

"Lady, you watch too much TV. This is back country up here."

She shot him a look and then finished unwrapping the leg. She didn't touch the injured area, not wanting a good kick from the horse. But she applied the ice pack and new wrapping, giving it a nice blue, bulging sock by the time she finished.

She sat back on her haunches and watched the horse test it. Then she straightened and brushed her hands off on the butt of her jeans. "I'll take that off in about twenty minutes."

Wheeler grunted. When she glanced up at him, she found him staring at her. A second passed—a very long second.

"I'm gonna muck out the stalls and scatter fresh bedding. Fill the feed bins. Why don't you go back to the front porch? Looks inviting."

They both looked that way. The porch was dark and sagging, far from inviting.

"Think I'll come into the barn with you," he said.

"Suit yourself."

Inside, she overturned a five-gallon bucket and patted it. "Get off that foot."

"You watch doctor shows too?" He gingerly lowered himself, careful of his foot.

"No" — she grinned — "but I played one on TV." She really hadn't. Her only claim to fame was this role on *Redemption Falls*. The kiss of death to actors was being typecast, but she couldn't imagine playing anything but a country girl. It was all she knew and if she thought on it, all she cared to.

Thankfully if Wheeler got the joke she'd just made, he didn't comment. While she shoveled out the stall, he watched her every move. She ignored him and got into the rhythm of work. Muscle memory had her finishing the job swiftly and efficiently. When she turned to Wheeler, she leaned on the pitchfork.

"Is it to your liking?" she asked.

To her surprise, his face turned a deep purple and he pushed to a stand, knocking over the bucket and almost losing a crutch.

She rushed forward to catch the object and kept it steady for him to take. With his eyes downcast, she wondered if he was trying to man up and hide the pain he was in.

"Look, I'll help you to the house. I really think you should have that foot up on a pillow."

He shook her off. "I got it."

She watched him limp back out of the barn and head to the house. Shaking her head at the general stubbornness of men, she returned to Gusto to check his leg. The ice had done a bit of its job, and the swelling seemed improved. She removed the ice and securely wrapped the leg again before taking one last look around the barn.

Everything seemed to be in order. No more chores for her to do.

There was only one thing left and that was leave.

In the house, Wheeler wasn't even sitting, let alone tending his injury. He was staring out the back window at what appeared to be birds at a feeder in the yard.

"All good with Gusto and the barn chores," she said.

He didn't turn.

Aria's heart dipped a little at the lack of response.

"Thank you," he said after a minute.

"Least I can do. I enjoyed the work. And…"

He turned his head and pierced her in his intense stare, shocking her so much she almost took a step back.

45

"Are you in pain?" she asked.

"No," he grated out. "Yes. But no."

"Okay, that makes no sense to me. But I'm going to take a leap here and ask you..."

He waited, his stare centered on her face.

"Look, I don't really have a place to go right now. And I'm not ready to go back to... where I came from. Would you mind if I stick around a bit longer? I can clean the floors or —"

"I'm not making you a slave, Aria. But if you need to stay a bit longer to figure out your next move, you're welcome."

Chapter Three

Goddammit, when was the last time Wheeler had found himself getting hard over a woman? Months. Hell, maybe years. It wasn't like he didn't love women — their lips, breasts, hips, legs... and what was between them. He just had other things to focus on than going out to bars to find someone to take to bed and later end up disappointed.

But watching Aria... Fuck, not only did she have built-in sex appeal but she knew her way around a horse, and that was sexy as hell.

He battled to get himself under control and turning away from the window was a difficulty because he was pitching a tent in these sweats.

Add in that her plea to stay was turning him inside out, and he could barely think of anything but what he'd do without these crutches and a bum foot.

Take her to bed.

Tumble her down and kiss those sweet bowed lips of hers.

Sink down into her.

He hardly knew the woman. He had to get the hell out of here before he regretted something.

Aria had gone back outside. When he stepped onto the porch, he found her leaning with her forearms on the railing, looking out over the mountains. Without turning, she said, "I love how your property rolls right up to the foothills."

"Yeah, it's somethin'." His gritty tone reflected only his lust and none of the sentimental shit he really felt about his land.

She pivoted her head to look at him. "Everything all right?"

"Yeah, I just gotta head over to my buddy's and see if I can do anything for him." He didn't — it was just the closest thing he could see to an exit.

Her brows pinched, and she drew away from the railing. "Oh. Do you want me to leave then?"

"Nah, just hang around if you want." *And be naked in my bed when I get back.*

He hurried as best he could down the steps. Lucky he could still drive since the break was on his left foot. Hell, to get away from her for a spell, he'd drive with the cast if he had to.

King's place was only a few miles off, and he was still half hard by the time he reached the gates of Blackwater. As he bumped to a stop before the garage, he took a moment to think on the past few days. It didn't even seem like his life.

He should be here right now, out with the herd or checking on King's new horse stock.

At this time of day, he knew his buddy would be hanging around the house, and sure enough, King had heard Wheeler's truck and rounded the barn. He nudged his hat up with a gloved fingertip and strode toward Wheeler, who fumbled his crutches out and managed to stay upright as he hit the ground.

"Everything all right?" King asked.

"Yeah, just had to get out for a bit. Wanted to see if there's anything I can do around here."

"Going stir crazy after only a few days, huh?" King gave him a crooked grin.

"You know it."

"Not a lot you can do for me with that." King gestured to his foot and the toes that were still sticking out, as he hadn't yet bothered with the footie.

"Yeah, I figured. I just..." How to explain finding a woman—and a sexy as hell one—in his barn and all that had come afterward?

"Can you make it to the porch? I'll grab us some water." As always, King had a way of knowing what was going on without being told. In this case, that Wheeler had something on his mind.

"Yeah, I reckon I can make it." He headed across the yard at a slow pace that King hung back for. When he finally settled into a chair on the porch, he did so with a sigh. "That's a lot harder than you'd think. I don't consider myself an unfit man, but that makes me wonder."

49

"You're using muscles you never used before. I'll get us that water." He went inside and a moment later stepped out with two bottled waters hooked in the fingers of one hand. They sat side by side sipping.

"It's nice to rest a spell. Bellarose has been up all night."

"Oh?" Wheeler cocked a brow.

"She's really upset. Something happened on the set of *Redemption Falls.*"

King's wife was an actor who'd spent time with King to learn about ranching and ended up becoming a rancher's wife. The pair couldn't be more suited for each other, and Wheeler was really happy for him. The set of the show wasn't far off, and she was able to live here at Blackwater and drive to work each morning while they were filming the show.

The publicity had many tourists coming to the area, and it made the townspeople happy, but luckily it hadn't touched Wheeler's world much. He liked to steer clear of that sort of thing.

King took a swig. "There's an actor on set who apparently took off when her boyfriend showed up with a surprise wedding for her. The dress, the minister, the flowers, you name it."

Wheeler's blood chilled like he'd just dumped the ice water straight into his veins. He lowered his bottle. "Wedding you say?"

"Yeah, I guess this woman couldn't face it all and took off, but nobody's heard from her and they're all very worried. The mountains tend to swallow people."

"Shit. Yeah." But in this case, the mountain hadn't swallowed the woman. Wheeler was pretty damn sure she was tucked up on his porch, safe and sound while staring at those mountains.

"I'm sure she's okay," he said. "Montana girl, isn't she?"

King jerked his stare to Wheeler. "How'd you know?"

Damn, he'd been called out. Shrugging, he said, "I read about her once and figured that's who you're talking about."

"Yeah, it is. There's a search party. The sheriff's on the case. Nobody saw which direction she went, so there's a lot of trails to follow."

Yeah, right to Wheeler's front door.

He set aside his bottle and got to his one foot with crutches in place. "I'd best be off. Thanks for the water."

"Already? Did you have something to talk about?"

"Nah, just felt the itch to come to Blackwater, I suppose. I'll go on home and prop up this foot."

"Looks like you need it. The toes are swollen."

Wheeler eyed him. "I've been told that. Thanks, man."

As he made his way back to the truck, his mind raced.

Aria was the actor off the show? And her fiancé had shown up with a surprise wedding? No wonder she'd made a break for it—Wheeler couldn't think of a worse surprise. Even being a man, he understood women enjoyed things like weddings and with no say in what was to become her special day…

Then again, it might have been more than the wedding ceremony that had her on the run. Maybe she hadn't been prepared to marry *that* man. Or any man. Wheeler got it. And now that he knew Aria's situation, he was more than happy to let her hide out at his place until she decided what to do.

It wasn't because she was the hottest thing he'd set eyes on in ages. Or that she was strangely easy to talk to, when he was often awkward with strangers.

No, none of those things.

However, she sure knew her way around a horse, and that surprised—and excited—him.

* * * * *

With too many worst-case scenarios playing in her head and enough energy to gallop all the way to Canada, Aria went back down to the barn to see what she could do to help Wheeler out.

It still stunned her that the man would allow a stranger to have free rein of his property with no question if she was trustworthy.

Or maybe it was just that he didn't have much of worth to steal. The place had loads of potential but needed some money to update. Even looking out at the land, the small barn and fenced area could be expanded to hold a lot more stock, if that was his desire.

She felt a bit grubby but hoped he wouldn't mind if she showered later. The dilemma of clean clothes was another thing. She couldn't exactly stay here for much longer—she needed to face her problems.

Whether or not her jilting Jason Lee had hit the media was a huge question mark as well. After all, he hadn't let the story slip that he'd proposed before she'd left for Washington. Was it possible that his embarrassment would keep him from saying more?

Then again, there were too many witnesses on the set of *Redemption Falls,* and it wouldn't be the first time an assistant or a crew member let a story leak out for a bit of side pay.

Tightening her lips over her teeth, she grabbed onto the fence and studied the horses. They either dozed or grazed. Three horses was almost laughable to a girl who'd grown up on a ranch for breeding, training and even sometimes boarding when times were lean. Her knowledge of horses extended far and wide, and her true love lay with the reining horses.

From the age of six, she'd wanted to compete to show off the skills and temperament of the horses she adored, but her father had seen her talent was in the training, and she had been encouraged to help with that as much as possible.

Which left her dream of competing unrealized, and that had been the first of many times a choice had been made for her. It was all downhill from there. Perhaps if she'd stood up to her daddy and explained how passionate she was about competing...

But she'd done a lot for the horses on the ranch, which was nothing to belittle. She was proud of those achievements as well.

Just as she was proud of becoming a handler on the set of *Redemption Falls*. And in some ways being thrown into acting as well. They were all accomplishments, even if she hadn't actively taken those paths in her life.

But I escaped what would have been a disaster of a marriage.

She was far from proud of how she'd gone about it. Now to get the gumption to face the damage she'd done and apologize to Jason.

She pushed off and leaped the fence, landing on her boots inside. The horses looked up at her, a bit wary of a stranger. As she approached Gusto, she crooned to him, talking in a low voice.

An inspection of his leg told her the ice had helped some, and though the horse had months of rehab to be whole again, at least it wasn't getting worse.

The horse was much like the man, watching her without reaction. When she reached out to stroke its neck, it stood there and accepted her touch, but she could tell it wasn't exactly happy to see her.

Yes, like Wheeler.

Maybe she should leave before he returned. He had enough on his platter without adding an actor who'd run away from more than a marriage she didn't want. At first, that had been the case, but after spending a few hours on Wheeler's small homestead... Well, she felt more alive than she had in a long time.

How long could she shirk her duties and ignore her contract? She was needed back on set, and she owed it to everyone to do her job to the best of her ability. Not to mention let them know of her whereabouts.

She inched closer to the horse, needing to smell it, lean into its solid warmth. She thought of Wheeler making his way down the mountain with a broken foot and the comfort Gusto must have been, even as the horse was his torment. He must have been seriously broken up by the injury and not knowing what the future would bring for the animal.

Gusto let her near, and she rested her forehead on his neck. Suddenly, her eyes were filled with tears. She wasn't a crier, and she hadn't shed a tear since running from Jason, which said a whole lot about how she felt for the man.

He deserved better. *She* deserved better than a one-sided relationship that would most likely land in the toilet like most celebrity marriages.

The tears didn't fall.

After a while, she moved away from Gusto and spent some time with each mare, talking to them and giving affection. Then she jumped the fence again and circled the barn, just inspecting everything.

It seemed to be in good repair, the wood solid and nothing like a protruding nail to catch a horse's flesh and tear it. Wheeler kept good care of his property. Even the house, though in need of updates, was kept in good repair, besides the porch steps. He was a man who had pride of ownership.

Noticing the hay in the barn was getting low, she found the dry stacks and hauled a few inside. Then she swept the space clean using an old broom with worn bristles and cleaned out the debris. After that, she oiled the tack hanging on the wall by the door.

By now, she was hungry again, but she hated to eat all of Wheeler's food. The man had little as it was, unless she broke out the contents of the freezer and grilled herself a steak.

Her stomach groaned at the thought of steaks with fried onions, but she couldn't do that.

The rumble of a truck engine brought her head up. She wiped her hands on the polishing cloth she was using on the tack and placed the cap back on the oil. When she stepped out of the barn, Wheeler was just planting his crutches beneath him. He must have caught her movement, because he turned his head to look at her.

She felt that gaze like a punch.

Oh no. Why was he looking at her that way? Like he was about to ask her a question she didn't want to answer.

He might have heard something about her.

She waited, fingers digging into the wood of the barn doorway.

"Gusto okay?" he asked as he neared.

"Yes, the swelling's gone down some."

He gave a nod. "Good. What have you been doing?"

She stepped aside to allow him to see the clean barn floor and to peek inside at the shining tack.

His hazel eyes held a hint of hesitation along with approval. "You didn't have to do that."

"You said as much, but I can't just sit still."

"I know the feeling." The corner of his lips twitched. Not quite a smile but it was far from the straight face of the man she'd met just that morning.

Lord, had it only been yesterday that she'd run from her own surprise wedding? It seemed like a month had passed.

"I was just about to have a water break. Care to join me?" she asked.

"Yeah, I'll take a glass and some pain pills."

She looked down at his foot. "Come on. You need that foot up and I won't take no for an answer."

"You mothering me?" Now the smile did emerge, like spring peeping out from under the snow and gray skies of winter. It reached up the sides of his face by way of smile lines to envelope the creases of his eyes.

The way that smile made her feel wasn't at all maternal but something very, very different.

As they made their way to the house again, Aria wished her mind would linger over the beauty of the mountains, the songbirds in nearby trees—anything but how Wheeler's smile made her feel more restless than she cared to admit.

She held the door open for him, and he went straight to the fridge.

"You don't drink the well water?" she asked.

"Well's only for backup. Mostly I run off a spring coming down from the mountain. It's good water, but King dropped off a case for me last time he stopped by."

She blinked at the name. It was familiar—and unlikely there were two men with the same name in the vicinity.

Wheeler handed her a water, and she took it with a quiet word of thanks.

"Speaking of King... I just heard some things from him."

"Who is King?" she managed, heart in her throat.

"I help him out on his cattle ranch, mostly with the horses now, as they're my skill set."

Oh God, it *was* the same King. The main actor of *Redemption Falls,* Bellarose's hubby.

He would definitely hear about what she'd done.

Wheeler stared at her. She met his gaze and slanted it away.

"He told me about an actor who ran away from her wedding."

Her mouth dried out.

"Maybe it's best if you start talkin'."

She gulped her water, and it went down the wrong tube. She coughed and water sprayed all over Wheeler's shirt and speckled his gray sweats, leaving dark spots. Abhorred, she continued to hack until she cleared her airway. Wheeler moved forward to smack her on the back.

He stepped toward her so quickly that his crutch hit the floor, and he had to brace a hand on the counter to keep from falling into her.

She sputtered to a stop, aware of how he hovered over her, so close.

"Let me get your crutch," she wheezed.

"I got it." Balancing on one foot, he crouched and grabbed the crutch, making it obvious that he'd done this same thing several times in the days since breaking his foot.

Once he had the crutch under him, he hobbled to the table. Aria continued to lean on the counter for support, wanting to run away — again.

He looked at her unwaveringly.

"It's me," she whispered.

"You're the runaway bride."

"I told you I was from the start."

"But not the part about the TV show. Why not?"

"You didn't recognize me, and I felt more at ease for it. It's bad enough that I ran, and more so that I ended up in a stranger's barn and now I'm mooching off his hospitality."

He grunted. "If mooching means caring for my stock and mucking out my stalls, tidying my barn and polishing my tack, then I'm good with being used."

An unexpected giggle escaped her.

Using the crutch, he nudged the chair leg, pushing it out from the table and inviting her to sit.

She did, folding her hands on the tabletop and trying to figure out how to explain or if she needed to at all.

Wheeler expected it of her. And maybe it would be a sort of release to spill the entire story?

"It's the horses I love the most," she began.

He raised a dark brow.

"I wasn't lying when I said I'm a Montana girl. Raised on a horse ranch and from a young age, my dad had me working with the stock, training them. We sold reining horses for competition."

"Good business."

The reining horses were ranch-type horses trained on their athletic abilities and competed within an arena. Many brought in a solid income if they were brought up right.

"Yes. But it was the competition I really wanted." She continued on, telling him of how she'd gotten onto the show but behind the scenes, and finally landing the acting gig. The money was good, the job not very demanding and she still got to be around horses.

"I met Jason at a mutual friend's party, and he called me right away."

"Jason?"

"Lee." She watched his face for recognition.

His eyes popped. "The action flick guy?"

Biting into her lower lip, she nodded. Her knuckles were nearly white from squeezing her fingers together.

"You ran out on the action flick guy?" His voice was laced with incredulousness.

Again, she nodded.

He let out a low whistle and sat back, looking at her.

She unclasped her hands and spread them. "Do you think I was wrong?"

"Honey, I don't know you, so how can I say? In my eyes, you must have run for a reason. Otherwise, wouldn't you have married the guy?"

"Yes," she said at once.

"Why did you say yes to his proposal in the first place?"

"I didn't exactly. It was just sort of… assumed on his part."

"But you didn't set him right."

"No. I was hoping things cooled down while I was here in Washington and then I'd find the words to say."

"So now what?"

She gave a light shake of her head. "I don't know. I can't hide forever, I know that."

"No."

"While I worked today, I thought of how to go back and talk to him. I can't really come up with anything yet."

"I understand how that would be hard. I avoid conflict any way I can, so I'm no good for advice."

"Well, don't we make a pair?" Her blurted statement had her face heating and him glancing away. Linking them in any way was a strange notion, and obviously one that neither wanted to think about.

"I'm sorry I didn't tell you from the start who I am."

He searched her eyes and then pushed to a stand. "Have you eaten since breakfast?"

"No."

"I'll make us something."

"No, I'm making it while you put that foot up." She pointed to the living room with a solemn expression she'd gotten from her mother and was told she was relatively good at executing.

With a chuckle, he shook his head. "Fine."

"Uhh… what should I make?"

"Some frozen pizzas left or if you get ambitious, steaks."

Her stomach grumbled. "Could we have the steaks for dinner?"

His lips twisted up at one corner. "Knock yourself out, honey."

After she started a pizza in the oven and laid out steaks to thaw, she put away the dry dishes, rooting around in his cupboards to find all their homes. When the timer dinged that the pizza was finished, she removed it using some ancient potholders. There wasn't a pizza wheel that she could locate, so she used a pair of scissors from the knife block.

He came in as she was cutting.

"What are you using—kitchen scissors?"

She half turned from the range. "Yes. Haven't you ever used them?"

"Only to cut a bit of twine or something, and never pizza. Seems like it's working."

She nodded. "My mom uses them to cut frozen pizzas. I didn't invent the technique."

She placed the pizza slices on two plates. "Why don't you go back into the living room to prop that foot and we'll eat in there?"

He groaned. "Again with the foot. Fine."

She followed him carrying both plates and grinning. He settled in a chair and she set the plates on the coffee table, a scarred, chunky oak that had seen better days but might be improved with a refinishing job. Then she returned to the kitchen for more drinks.

When they were each halfway through their slices, she spoke up. "You know Bellarose I'm assuming."

"Stood up for their wedding." He swiped his tongue over his lip, gathering sauce.

Aria's body seemed to dial up some internal thermometer, heating her insides.

"King's one of my best friends. Every day I work on his ranch, I come home and feel I've failed with my own place."

She lowered her slice to her plate, staring at him. "Your dream is to have more than a few horses?"

He lifted a shoulder in a shrug. "Dunno. I enjoy working with them but haven't given a lot of thought to more. Is that lazy of me?"

"Not if what you're doing makes you happy."

He set down his own slice, leaning forward on his seat and piercing her in his gaze. "What makes you happy?"

She eyed him. "Not getting married?"

They burst out laughing.

* * * * *

Aria hovered over Wheeler. She was staring at his foot, but he couldn't tear his gaze from her hair, the way it fell in a wave across her shoulder. The ends reached for her perky breasts.

Annnd just like that, I'm hard.

He stirred inside his sweats, his cock stretching an inch the longer she stood there looking at his foot.

"Does it hurt you?" she asked.

"Not much." He was lying—it throbbed like a bitch.

She must have heard something in his voice, because she focused on his face. "No wonder you're in pain. You were on it too much today."

"It's just a foot."

"Is that what you say about your horse?"

She grabbed a cushion that was rather flat from years of use and gently slipped a hand under his calf.

He gritted his teeth. It'd been far too long since he'd experienced a woman's soft touch, and the warmth of her fingers permeated the cloth of his sweats. She lifted his leg and placed the cushion on the footstool, and then lowered his foot to it.

She giggled. "Didn't do much, did it?"

"Those pillows are circa '87 by my guess. The fluff's out of them."

She giggled again. "Do you have an extra bed pillow to use?"

"Sure. I'll grab one." He moved to stand, but she waved him back and was off before he could call her back. As he listened to her retreating footsteps, he pictured her—how her body moved with each step and the way her hair swung on her back.

He closed his eyes briefly on the memory of how her breasts bounced lightly, and he battled with his growing erection, which he couldn't hide if he kept thinking this way. He'd just about mastered his mind when he it occurred to him Aria was in his bedroom.

His cock popped to full mast, and he shoved it down, tucking it the best he could so he wasn't tenting his sweats again. If she was still here in the morning, he'd find an old pair of jeans and slit the leg to get his cast through it.

When she returned carrying one of his plump bed pillows, he caught a faint flush to her cheeks.

"You have a washer and dryer? You have a lot of dirty laundry."

"Oh." So that was why she was blushing—his wadded up laundry that had mostly missed the basket the past few days was probably offensive to a sweet woman who didn't even do her own menial chores.

"Yeah, through the kitchen there's a mud porch and the facilities are out there."

"I'll get a load started in a minute." She bent over him again, and God, he had to restrain himself from curling his fingers around her arm and reeling her in. He hadn't felt such a balls-out chemical lust as he had right this minute with Aria. Until now he'd always wondered how one-night stands happened.

Now he knew.

She grabbed his leg again sooner than he realized he should lift it himself, and she plumped the cushion before gently placing his foot down.

"That's a little better." She turned brown eyes on him. But they weren't just brown. They reminded him of a horse's coat in the sunshine, rippling as it moved with shades of chestnut and chocolate and hints of copper.

"It's fine," he managed gruffly.

"Do you need something before I start on the laundry?"

"You don't need to do that. I can manage it fine."

"I have no doubt you'd rig up some way of hauling baskets to the laundry room. Maybe with a rope and harness system?" She grinned down at him. "But there's no reason for you to do it if I can help."

"But why *are* you helping? I'm nothing to you."

She gaped at him a moment. "It's true we're strangers. But I'd help a stranger along the road who needed assistance, and I'd say by now, you're working into acquaintance territory."

Her words shouldn't touch him, but they did, heating him smack in the center of his chest. "As long as you don't feel beholden because you slept in my barn."

"Okay, I won't. I'll think of it as a gift to you."

His brow shot up.

A teasing light came to her eyes. "It's not every day that I gift someone with my presence and sleep in their barn stall."

His lips quirked at one corner. "You can have the couch tonight if you do real a real nice folding job."

Her eyes twinkled. "Thanks." She started to move away.

"But Aria." He snagged her wrist before she could take a step.

She stared down at his fingers on her skin, and damn if he wasn't on fire for her all over again. So delicate, feminine… fragile. She could be injured by one of his big quarter horses so easily.

Their gazes collided and held. Under his fingertip, her pulse hammered against the soft skin.

"You're missing and you have to tell someone soon where you're at."

"You didn't tell King, did you?" Amazement slid across her eyes.

He shook his head. "Isn't my secret to tell. But you've gotta put their minds at ease. There are people who care about you."

Biting her lip, she nodded. "You're right. But maybe I won't tell them where I'm at, just that I'm all right. If I could only stay a few more days..."

Christ, he'd never live through several days with this woman in his house, mothering him over his foot and helping out with everything from dishes, laundry and cooking to polishing tack.

How could he turn away from the silent plea in her big brown eyes?

"Stay," he heard himself grate out.

Her eyes widened.

"But use the phone to call someone, okay?" Realizing he still held her by the wrist, he gave a mental command for his fingers to uncurl and release her.

She stepped back. "I have my cell on me but—"

"No service," he finished. "Only if you get out to the end of the road. There you can get a bar if skies are clear. But I've got a landline for that reason."

"And no internet."

He chuckled. "What would a man like me do with internet?"

"Look up ways to be more stubborn about getting help after breaking your foot?"

Her sassy remark yanked a laugh from deep inside him, and it shoved free like an unbroken horse through a gate. She smiled in response, and he wondered how he'd ever lived alone before finding her this morning.

Acquaintances, hell. Did people want to strip their acquaintances, peel off their clothes and kiss every inch of their skin?

To cover his mind's wanderings, he adjusted his foot atop the pillow. "Thank you, Aria. But you're wrong about me looking up ways to be more stubborn. I come by that honest."

She braced a hand on the arm of his chair and leaned down close, so close that he could palm the back of her head and pull her in for a kiss. Her eyes were bright, her gaze direct as she said, "I'm stubborn too. Let's see who gets their way."

Then she straightened and sashayed from the room to collect his laundry.

He watched her go, hard as stone and aching in more places than his foot.

Chapter Four

The morning dew was just burning off, rising from the ground in wisps of fog, making Aria think of fairies. As a little girl, she used to love looking out of her bedroom window at the same thing in her own fields and dreaming of what worlds could live in the tall grasses under the cloak of the fog.

Sprites and fairies for sure, but also an entire peeper frog clan who fought for their territory against the otherworldly beings.

She smiled at the pretend play of the child she'd been. Dreaming wasn't only something for the young, though—it was for all ages. Her dreams had just changed.

She just wasn't entirely sure what they were at the moment. She wasn't a woman to do a job halfway, so returning to the set of *Redemption Falls* was her first goal.

Right after talking to Jason.

She fisted her hand and tapped it against her lips. Each time she tried to come up with words to explain, her mind blanked. It might as well be that white fog rising from the grass.

Maybe it was years of going along with things that was making her so indecisive now. But she couldn't remain this way for long. After all, she'd made the choice to run from her wedding and that came with consequences—like cleaning up her mess.

How easy it was to throw herself into work she enjoyed, something she could do with her eyes closed. Was it horrible to want mindless tasks for a while? To float along and let life unravel?

That's how I got here in the first place.

She turned for the barn and the horses heard her, eagerly snorting and shifting in their stalls for what they knew was coming. Today she had a wrinkled apple she'd found in a fruit basket in the kitchen and sliced it for them. She was just reaching the first mare's stall when the low rumble of an engine reached her ears.

She stood and went back out, heart pounding in her throat and making her feel queasy. If someone had discovered she was hiding out here…

A truck came into view, trundling up the driveway. Aria clung to the door frame, keeping her head ducked out of sight in case.

In case of what? She couldn't possibly run again. That was a child's tactic, and she was not a child. Though she'd made the mistake once already, she wasn't very proud of it.

A glance toward the house showed her Wheeler had stepped onto the porch. While he made his slow way down the steps, the truck pulled to a stop. A cowboy with a black hat climbed out, and she recognized him immediately as King Yates, Bellarose's husband. Their wedding photos were plastered all over the world.

It was impossible to work with Bellarose and not take an interest in the woman's life, though Aria was still quite shy with the other actors. Bellarose seemed to make more attempts than most to speak to Aria, almost taking her under her wing. Aria appreciated it more than she had ever revealed.

When King closed the truck door, he lifted a hand in greeting to Wheeler. The pair met halfway across the yard, and Aria inched out a bit to watch them. Wheeler threw a look her way but if he spotted her, he didn't show it.

King hooked his thumb in his jeans pocket and Wheeler leaned on his crutch, taking the weight off his broken foot. She watched him closely, how he pulled at his hat brim as he talked. Did he even notice he did that? And how he turned every so often to look out over the mountain, as if he'd find some answer there.

Aria might be new to acting, but she was learning to watch people closely to gather mannerisms that would help her later in her role. Though currently, she didn't find herself very challenged.

Another engine noise startled her, and she sucked in a breath as she stared at the drive. Another truck came over the rise, this one white. As that driver parked, King and Wheeler made their way toward the barn.

Heart pounding hard and fast, Aria wondered what to do now. She could stick around and meet King and this new guy, who she saw was the vet now that he took a toolbox from his truck and headed her way.

She wasn't ready to rejoin the world just yet. She needed to remain hidden a while longer.

She slipped out the back into the fenced area and ducked under the rail. When the guys came in the front, she circled the building and made a break for the well-beaten path leading to the foothills. Wheeler must take regularly trail rides by this route, and she could see why it would be a beautiful ride.

Taking long strides and pulling in breaths of the fresh air into her lungs felt good, and before she knew it, she'd begun the climb. The trail forked off and she took the left branch. In seconds, the path grew steep. Wheeler couldn't take the horses this direction. The exercise felt good and the blood pumping through her system helped clear her head a bit.

When she began breathing hard, she found an open spot to sit and curled her legs to her chest to enjoy the solitude.

She wondered what the vet had to say about the injury. She hoped the horse was making improvements. The thought of Gusto being put down gave her a sharp pang. It would be a hard blow to Wheeler if such a thing was necessary.

Also, would Wheeler tell King about her being on his ranch? He was right that she needed to tell people so they didn't worry about her.

A thought occurred to her, and she pulled out her cell phone from her pocket. The battery was low and there was still no service here, so she switched it off and repocketed it.

She made a mental list of who to contact. Her parents, her producer, Dickson. Jason, of course... Bellarose? She'd hold off on that. She didn't exactly have a close relationship with the woman, but the fact that she'd spent the night upset by Aria's disappearance left a brick weight in her chest.

So yes, she'd contact Bellarose.

Resting her head on her knees, she thought of Jason and what he must be feeling. She had hurt him, and she felt awful. Everything about her actions left her aching and remorseful.

Everything since that moment had been much easier — working with Wheeler's horses, helping him out. Maybe she was making amends for her mistakes, even in a small way.

Or I just plain ole like being here.

The wind started to cut through her top, and she got up. Back on the path, she considered what she'd do if King and the vet hadn't left, but she didn't need to decide because the trucks were gone when she entered the clearing.

75

She went up to the house and found Wheeler in the mud room, balanced on one foot and sans crutches, pulling clothes from the dryer into a basket on the floor.

Hearing her, he threw a look over his shoulder. "You could toss your clothes in the wash too."

She glanced down at her grubby shirt and jeans she'd slept in twice and worked in plenty. "I'd love to, but what will I put on?"

"I got some clean sweats and T-shirts. Be big on you but get you through while yours are washed."

"A shower sounds amazing."

"Go on." His voice was deep, rough. It sandpapered over her senses, leaving behind a ripple of awareness inside her.

Today he wore a black T-shirt and an open flannel over it, and he'd sliced the leg of a pair of holey denim jeans. Through a rip under the back pocket, she saw he wore red boxers. But the thing that was really getting to her, working under her skin in all the strange ways men had to entice a woman... was the fact that he hadn't shaved today.

Sporting a thick black shadow on his jaw and upper lip, he had her twisting her fingers together.

He cast another look her way. "I got this. Why don't you jump in the shower?"

"Too stinky for ya?" She laughed, only half kidding.

"I've spent years on roundup with guys who don't wash in a month. The sweat of one woman's not gonna affront my senses."

She caught a gleam in his eye.

"You can tell me about the roundup when I get out. And what the vet said."

"Will do."

She left him and went into the 1980s bathroom. Turning on the water and shedding her clothes shouldn't feel like such a delicious pleasure, but it kind of made her stop taking for granted the luxuries she had in life.

The hair and makeup artists, the wardrobe people and all those who washed her dirty clothes, did her dishes and put food in front of her, she was grateful for each and every one. She wasn't spoiled as some celebrities were, but she never wanted to become that way either. She must make it a point to let them know how valuable their time was to her.

The thought of giving them little gifts too excited her when she returned to the set.

Not yet, but soon.

And Jason deserved an explanation and apology.

The bodywash she used smelled masculine and spicy, reminding her of all the guys in her life she'd spent time with, and she didn't mind. She dug her fingers into her scalp to scrub her hair and then rinsed the shampoo from it. There was no conditioner, but she'd deal with the tangles.

After the shower, she felt more human. Looking at her discarded dirty clothes made her wrinkle her nose. No way did she want to put those back on. She wrapped herself in a towel and went to the door to call out to Wheeler for the sweats and T-shirt he'd mentioned, when there was a knock.

She cracked the door a couple inches.

He loomed there on crutches, holding a wad of clothes in one hand. His gaze traveled over her wet, tangled hair to the slope of her bare shoulders and down to the towel, banded tight above her breasts.

His gaze tumbled down the towel to her bare thighs. Lingered. Then slowly came back up.

Whoa. What is that?

Liquid warmth spread over her like a glaze of frosting over a cake fresh from the oven. At recognition of his interest, her core gave a throb.

"Here ya go." His voice was more than gritty this time—it sounded as though he'd gulped a fifth of whiskey between doing laundry and coming to the bathroom door with clothes for her.

She reached out, one hand latched to the towel to keep it closed around her nudity.

A strange urge hit her. What if she just shoved back the door and dropped the towel? Let Wheeler push her up against the dated blue vanity and rub that beard scruff all over her?

He didn't put the clothes into her hand, and she didn't take them. They just stared at each other.

Heartbeats passed while a new pulse took up residence between her thighs, leaving her skin sticky with her juices.

A trickle of a breath passed her lips. He ran his tongue across his own.

Suddenly, he shoved the clothes at her. "Get dressed."

She fielded the clothes, nearly dropping them, and closed the door again. Leaning against the vanity, her heart tripping wildly, she whispered, "What was that?"

Never in her life had she felt a profound urge to give herself to a man. She was modest to the extreme, and it had taken Jason months of patience before she'd finally given into his advances.

She'd known Wheeler less than two days, and she was thinking about how it would feel for him to lift her onto the vanity edge and plunge his cock into her?

With shaking hands, she dropped the towel. Her nipples were distended and aching, and her clit in the same state. She hadn't masturbated in a long time, but maybe she needed to in order to clear her thoughts of fantasies of Wheeler.

It didn't help when she slid his big sweats over her bare pussy and knotted the strings to hold them in place. Even then, they sagged low on her hips. And his shirt smelled of fresh laundry and a hint of the owner. Both of these things only heightened her arousal.

By the time she brushed out her hair and toweled the droplets of water from the ends again, she barely had a grip on herself. She really had lost her mind, hadn't she? First the Jason thing and now this?

* * * * *

Jesus Christ. Wheeler's jeans were doing nothing to harness the erection he sported after getting a good eyeful of that gorgeous, damp and dewy woman clad in nothing but his towel.

Fuck, he wanted to storm back there, part her thighs and drop down and taste her. The slickness of her pussy against his tongue, hearing her throaty cries as he gave her orgasm after orgasm...

He smacked a palm off his forehead to snap himself out of it. It didn't fucking help.

He plopped onto the footstool in the living room. Using a crutch, he nudged the laundry basket closer and began folding garments with rapid precision. Left, right, up, stack. Left, right, up, stack.

The sound of the bathroom door opening might as well have been a gunshot with the way he reacted, half coming off the footstool. Then he made the mistake of looking up to see Aria standing there wearing his sweats, loose and hanging off her rounded hips and his All American Rodeo T-shirt knotted at her waist. She cradled her clothes in one arm, and the action made her top ride up on that side to reveal more of that golden tan, freshly showered skin.

A glance at her clothing parcel just about gave him a fucking heart attack, because he caught the barest hint of lavender lace that must be her panties or bra.

Somebody call a priest. I have a confession to make for a sin I haven't even committed yet.

Taking somebody else's fiancé, spreading her out on his bed and fucking her for the next twenty-four hours solid was surely something he'd spend eternity in hell for.

His mind stuttered to a halt. Wait—she wasn't somebody's fiancé anymore, was she?

Hell, he was in the clear.

"I see you managed to move the basket."

"Yeah, the damn crutches are good for somethin'." He sounded ornerier than he felt, but that was just his very full, distended balls being squashed in his jeans.

"I'll just put these in the wash." She drifted off, and he had to twist to watch her go. God, those sweats were hardly staying in place. One move and they'd slip down to show the curves of what he imaged to be her bare cheeks.

Turning around again, he rubbed his hand over his face. What had he gotten himself into? All he did was find her asleep in the straw, answered her plea to

81

stay a day or two and figure things out while helping him at a low point in his life. And now… now he was having filthy, dirty fantasies about her involving some rope and a lot of lube.

He managed to wad up a couple pairs of jeans in the bottom of the basket in the time she was gone. When she poked her head around the doorway, he looked up. Her hair was starting to dry in loose waves, making her look even more like a swimsuit model.

"Mind if I make that phone call now?" she asked softly.

"Of course not."

"It's long distance."

"I can manage the bill."

She shot him a smile and vanished again. He tried to focus on the laundry and then gave up and sat there, wishing he wasn't laid up, the vet hadn't told him it would take up to nine months to heal Gusto's strained ligament and that he knew what to do with the woman using his phone.

A damn celebrity right here, hiding out from her world. Of course, he hadn't known that from the start, but now he couldn't help but feel he was doing something wrong in letting her stay.

When King and the vet both had commented on what good care Wheeler was taking of the horse's injury, he'd felt damn bad about remaining silent on the matter. He wasn't one to take credit for something he didn't do, but Aria had been nowhere to be found when they entered the barn.

He wasn't surprised really, finding her gone. He'd have to ask where she'd taken herself off to.

Plus, he didn't like lying to King. His friend had come to hear what the vet had to say so he could help Wheeler out, and here Wheeler was keeping important information from him.

He hoped after Aria made her long-distance call that she'd make a few to the people who worked with her on the set and let them know she wasn't curled up under a rock on the mountain with hypothermia from being in the elements for several days.

No, she's here in my house, cooking and cleaning for me and wearing my T-shirt.

He got up and used the crutch to nudge the basket out of the way. His toes were looking better from propping his foot, even if he didn't want to admit staying off it was best. Six more weeks of this would kill him. Somehow, he had to find a way to shove the thing into a cowboy boot and get on with his life.

A sniffling sound drew his head up and around. He stared at the place where Aria had disappeared. He couldn't make out her words but he knew when a woman was emotional.

Shifting the crutches under his arms, he rocked forward to go to her and then stopped himself. She needed her privacy. But did she need a kind word, human comfort? He hadn't realized he did until she showed up here.

"Bye, Daddy." Her voice carried to Wheeler. He busied himself with punting the laundry basket around some more to appear that he wasn't eavesdropping. When she entered the living room, her eyes were watery.

"You okay?" he asked.

She nodded. "Apparently, the show's producer released a statement this morning that I had been missing for twenty-four hours, and my parents were pretty freaked out."

"Damn. It means the sheriff will be searching for you."

"I've made a huge mess of things." She twisted her fingers before her. "I'm not sure what to do or where to start."

"I'll handle the sheriff and he can tell the people you work with."

She nodded. "I'd appreciate it. I never thought about how many people would be upset by my actions. I was only reacting. I felt caged, cornered, trapped."

"Like a wild animal," he filled in.

She met his stare. "Exactly. I didn't know what to do to get out of that situation, and I made a snap decision that I'm now regretting very much."

Her tone of despair called out to him, and he swung himself forward, planting himself in front of her. "We all make radical choices at times."

"That doesn't sound like you."

He chuckled. "I wasn't always old before my time."

She cocked her head. "Is that what you think of yourself?"

He considered what he'd said. "Guess I feel it's circumstances or somethin'. Hell, I don't know. We're not talking about me—you're projecting onto me."

That brought a laugh from her, a tinkling, musical sound that gripped him hard. "Maybe I am projecting."

"Okay, when a squirrel runs up a tree and gets cornered by a dog, what's it do?"

Her brows shot up. "Jump?"

"Yep, to the next tree."

"You're telling me to run again? I wonder if your neighbor will enjoy my company as much?"

"No, I'm not telling you to run, and who said I don't enjoy your company? I'm saying find a way to get out of the situation. First way is by calling everyone and tell them you're somewhere safe, laying low for a week or so until—"

"A week?" Her eyes shone.

He stopped to look at her, face fresh and devoid of makeup, hair starting to dry around her temples.

"You're saying I can stay for a week?"

"Well, King and the vet did say you did a fantastic job getting the swelling down on Gusto's leg." Though she had made something else swell a whole lot more, and Wheeler was even now suffering the effects of it.

"Will you really call the sheriff for me?"

"Yes, but you gotta make the rest of the calls."

"Okay."

They stared at each other. "I could use some coffee. Would you mind making a pot while I call the sheriff's office?" he asked.

Ten minutes later, he had the situation under control. Search parties that were about to be called out were stopped in time, and he even was promised a hand of poker with the guys soon.

"Thank you," she said as soon as he entered the kitchen.

He dipped his head in a nod.

"It seems like I owe everyone an explanation."

"It probably feels pretty daunting." He looked at her slumped shoulders.

"Yeah. But it's time I take some control. I've let things happen around me for too long. If you don't mind, I'd like some help getting in touch with Bellarose."

He jerked his head up. "I can make that happen."

"Thank you. It's just that she's been kind to me in the past, and my disappearing is no way to repay that."

"We can head up there tomorrow if you'd like."

"She'll be on set until seven."

"Good time to break out the drinks, then."

She smiled, looking a bit more at ease. "You've been... well, great, Wheeler."

He snorted. "All I've done is provide some bedding for you to sleep in."

"Much more than that. Why did you help me?"

He stared at her for a long moment. Was it possible for her to grow prettier by the hour? With the light from the window behind her that way and her hair trailing in thick ribbons over her shoulders...

"I might have run a time or two in my life," he blurted out.

"Whoa. You? Sit and have some coffee and tell me all about it."

He chuckled at her tone of voice, which had taken on that of a talk show host.

He slipped into the chair while she brought him a mug of steaming brew. Then she sat across from him and clasped her hands on the table, eyes eager.

"All right, I suppose you've told me some about you, so it's my turn."

"Yes."

"It's nothing nearly so exciting as being a celebrity who's just fled from her own wedding."

Aria let out a groan that was too soft and enthralling to do anything but arouse the hell out of him. He was glad to be sitting down and under cover of the table.

"Before I got into wrangling, I rodeo'd a while."

"What event?"

"Bronc ridin'."

She nodded, eyes on his face. "I can see that."

"Yeah, well, I wasn't very good at it. I was better at the behind the scenes stuff, tending horses, helping out, giving advice."

"So you ran from that?"

He gave a short laugh. "Hardly something to run from. I ran from a woman."

"Ah."

"It was short-lived, two months tops. I was young and dumb and hadn't realized yet that there are women out there chasing the next buckle. She left me on the hook, went off with one of my buddies at the time."

Aria released a low whistle. "Did you love her?"

"Fancied myself in love, I suppose. But isn't everyone in love when they're eighteen?"

She nodded. "What happened?"

"I was pissed, in a rage actually, when I found out they'd spent the night together. I channeled the energy into my ride and came out with the top score. I was moving on to the next round."

"That's exciting."

"It was. Except it no longer mattered to me. She had taken something that had once meant a lot and cheapened it. The minute she saw my score, she was all over me, huggin' on my neck and... Well, you can imagine."

"Yes."

"In that moment I wondered what the hell I was even doing with my life. So before I got that buckle, I walked out to my truck and drove away. Never looked back."

"You ran from the awards ceremony?"

"Yeah, and to this day I don't really regret it."

She lifted her own mug to her lips. Over the rim, she said, "I don't see how this story's supposed to help me. You ran and don't have regrets and I ran and I do."

His lips twisted upward. "Never said I'm good at storytelling. Just told you I ran once myself and that's the tale. Maybe what I'm saying is that someday you'll look back at this moment and it won't feel so terrible. You might even feel relief that you got yourself out of a situation that would have ended badly."

"Like you did with that woman."

He nodded. "Nothin' but heartache in that relationship, and I wasn't going to stick around for more."

"I guess our stories are the same, then. I couldn't see how marrying a man I don't love was going to make me — or either of us — happy."

They sipped in companionable silence.

"Wheeler."

He met her stare.

"If you had to do it again, would you have done it differently?" she asked.

"Only thing I would have done differently, honey, is not broken my foot or injured my horse this week. How 'bout you?"

Chapter Five

"Wait a minute." Wheeler was on his third cup of coffee and Aria didn't know how the man wasn't jittery as a chicken in a wolf's den. He leaned across the table, dark eyes probing hers. "You're telling me that the character you play returned to her family's ranch from the South after falling in love with her brother?"

"Stepbrother," she corrected, hiding her smile in her mug.

He sat back abruptly, spine hitting his chair and leg kicked out to the side. "That's fucked up."

Aria had grown up around rough men with rougher mouths, and she couldn't help but compare the one in front of her to those guys who'd worked on her family's ranch. Then compare them to people like Jason Lee. It wasn't that the man was awful in any way. He just wasn't her type.

There—she'd said it. Or rather, she'd finally pinpointed her reason for never quite connecting with him.

She hadn't realized she'd frozen in place until Wheeler sat forward and waved a hand in front of her face. "You okay?"

She nodded. "Just thinking."

"About how fucked up that entire script is, yeah, I get it." He stood and carried his mug to the sink. It was amazing how much skill he was getting on those crutches.

And how totally freakin' hot he was. He leaned over the sink, and she latched her stare onto his backside, all carved planes of muscle that would flex when he got into the saddle.

When she gripped it in the throes of lust.

She quickly stood and carried her own mug to the sink. "I've drank more coffee than I have since I was a kid and used to sneak it."

"Amateur." His eyes danced.

Her breath caught.

A long moment passed while they stood close to each other but without speaking. There seemed to be no need to when her body had plenty to say. Beneath his T-shirt, her nipples puckered at the thought of brushing them against his chest as she went on tiptoe and kissed those hard lips.

Purely to see if they were as hard as they looked, of course.

His gaze fell over her lips, and the mere look held her in place. Her feet were bolted to the floor.

"You know, Aria, you have to go back to your life."

She rooted her stare on his mouth as well. "I know."

"I can manage fine."

"I know. But I thought I was invited to stay for a week?"

He let out a sound like a groan. "I won't last a week, honey."

Her gaze shot to his. A noise escaped her too, and then somehow, she was in his arms, crushed between that steely body and the ugly baby blue countertop. Her first thought was how coarse his five o'clock shadow was on her skin, right before he sucked everything from her mind with his kiss.

When she brought her hands to his face and strained upward, one of his crutches hit the floor. They ignored the sharp bang, and Wheeler took that moment to swipe his tongue over the seam of her lips.

On a fevered gasp, she opened to him. He plunged inside, hot, wet and all-consuming. She fought her way closer, needing to feel him wrapped all around her. He locked an arm around her waist and bent her to him, giving her an up-close-and-personal knowledge of how big, thick and hard his cock was.

She wiggled against it, and he growled low in his throat. Sweeping the interior of her mouth with his tongue once, twice. By the fifth stroke, she was ready to strip for him, walk him back to the chair and straddle him right here in the kitchen.

"Fucking hell," he grated out.

"Until a few minutes ago, I didn't realize how much I love a man with a dirty mouth." She nipped at his lower lip.

His grin spread under her teeth. "Fuck yeah."

With a hand hooked around his nape, she brought him back to her mouth, kissing him as hard as he gave, matching him swipe for swipe and trading bites until she quaked for more.

"Aria." He drew back to look into her eyes.

"Wheeler." Her breasts rose and fell with her gasping breaths.

"If I take you once, I won't stop. You'd best walk away."

She reached for his shirt buttons. "What if I won't walk away?"

"Then you'd better walk to my bedroom right now, before I pick you up and carry you there myself, broken foot and all."

She threw him a wink. "Can't have you straining that foot, now."

With that, she turned and walked off, making sure to give him an inviting look. A second later, she heard him cuss and the noise of the crutches on the floor, fast on her trail.

* * * * *

Jesus, Wheeler was harder than pure iron and getting harder by the second. Aria turned to him the

94

minute he walked through the door and kissed him. Her plump lips crushed against his couldn't even be reality, could it? He must have fallen off his crutches and hit his damn head. No way was this happening.

Except she felt real enough, all soft, silky curves against his, and she tasted like heaven.

He dropped a crutch and walked her backward to his bed. Her knees hit the edge and she dropped to it, working at his buttons till his shirt hung open. He peeled it off, leaving him in only a T-shirt and jeans.

Seated on his mattress that way, gazing up at him with stars in her eyes and her lips red and swollen from his kisses, she was the most gorgeous and sensual creature ever to walk the earth.

Passion struck him as he eased his fingers into her hair above her ear. He threw down his other crutch and lifted her easily, moving her up the bed and cloaking her with his body in one swift move.

He wrenched the hell out of his foot but the only pain he acknowledged was in his groin. Each throb of his heart had his cock pounding, pushing against his jeans so hard that he couldn't take much more of this torment.

"You're so goddamn beautiful. Give me your mouth." His command pulled a rasp from her, and her eyelids hooded a split second before he captured her mouth again. Need struck him hard, and he let his hips drop, sinking against her. While they kissed, he reached under her top, finding her smooth stomach.

When he breached the spot where her bra should be, he went still, puffing hard for control.

"No bra."

"It's in the wash." She yanked the shirt over his head. "God, you're built."

"Hard work." In a swift movement, he tore her top off too and cast it aside. Her hair, still damp in spots, spread over his bed in a fan that he wanted to bury his nose in.

Later. Right now her little rosy nipples were begging for his lips. Teeth, tongue.

He dropped his head and took one tight bud between his lips, working it back and forth while she moaned and arched upward for more. Her little noises were driving him wild. He sucked her nipple into his mouth and rolled his tongue around the puckered edges.

She dug her nails lightly into his scalp, guiding him. He released her with a slick pop and moved to the other breast, trailing his rough jaw from one mound to the other.

"Wheeler!" She yanked him down to her nipple, and he realized with a jolt that she didn't just like nipple play — she seemed to love it. So sensitive to his touch, she allowed him to worship each for long minutes. He sucked and bit into each juicy bud until he was about to blow. Still, he wanted to give her more and more.

"You'd better have condoms," she rasped.

"A cowboy's always prepared."

She flashed a grin and stretched her fingers low over his abs. When she dipped a fingertip under his belt, he felt the vibrations all the way to the toe of his lone boot.

All he could say was thank God he wasn't in a body cast and could still move his hips.

Spattering kisses over her throat and the shell of her ear, he let her flip open his belt and pop the button of his jeans. The zipper…

"Christ," he hissed out.

Just short of her touching him, he stopped her with a hand on her wrist. He pinned her in his stare. Then he kissed her.

She squeaked out a gasp, and he didn't let up, assaulting her with thrusts of his tongue and pinching her nipples. When he could barely hold back another second, he ventured south.

Under the elastic of the sweats she wore. Down, down, until his fingers met silky, bare skin.

Then wet folds.

Soaking wet.

In one rough jerk, he leaned upward and yanked his sweats down her hips. One glance at the shape of her plump pussy lips and the glistening seam had him growling for more.

"I'm going to eat this sweet pussy until you can't stop begging me for more." He parted her thighs and dived between them, mouth open wide over her pussy.

She cried out. He moaned into her swollen flesh and probed the seam with the tip of his tongue, traveling down to taste all her arousal and then back up until he bumped her distended clit.

Writhing under him, he trapped her ass in his hands and lifted her to his mouth. Watching her face as he devoured her, inch by inch, sucking and lapping while she locked her gaze onto his.

Hell, he'd never been with a woman like this before. Not only was the heat level off the charts and he harder than he'd ever been, but the goddamn intimacy of that look they shared was driving him mad.

He wanted more. So much more.

He sucked on her nubbin, and she bowed in his hands, digging her heels into the mattress to rub herself on his tongue. He locked her in his gaze and opened his mouth wide to gave her his whole tongue. She fucked up and down it, sliding on a slippery path to heaven or hell. One of them was burning up, and it was going to be her first.

He had to hold out.

Easing his fingers up her thigh, damp with juices, he circled her wet center. She hummed in pleasure, and he took that a step further, adding a fingertip to her backside.

She went still. And then jerked hard against him. "Wheeler. So close. So…"

"Mmm." He licked her pretty slit up and down while stretching her with his first two fingers and teasing her netherhole with the third. Her inner thighs clenched around his ears, toned from riding and working out as she must to keep in shape for the camera.

Her lips parted on a silent gasp. Beneath the point of his tongue, he felt her clit tense, the bundle of nerves beginning to tremor. Then the first tight squeeze of her inner walls around his fingers had him pushing her faster, harder, demanding what he wanted from her, and he wouldn't let her back down.

The bed trembled under her ecstasy. She pushed upward onto her elbows, watching him claim her sweetness for his own. To his surprise, she parted her thighs more, and the movement drew him into her. All three of his fingers sank to the knuckles and wild heat enveloped his hand as she came apart in sharp jerks of her hips and feminine cries.

* * * * *

Aria's first words that came to mind were *fucking hell.*

Never had she reached heights like that, and definitely not with a man.

Maybe it was the demanding way Wheeler stared straight into her eyes while he tongued and fingered her. Or that surprise he'd given her by claiming her ass as well. She was a virgin in that sense, and the idea of anybody touching her there had given her hesitation, so nobody had ever tried to persuade her further.

But Wheeler hadn't asked — he'd just taken.

Her insides still throbbed with tiny aftershocks that he pulled from her with soft flicks of his tongue across her pussy lips and clit. When he drew his fingers from her body, he delved his tongue into her pussy and lapped up all the juices she'd spilled. Again, something that she'd never experienced.

She fisted the covers and watched him, unable to tear her gaze from him. The expression he wore... like he was loving every minute of pleasuring her... it gave her a warm thrill deep in her belly.

The entire encounter felt surreal. One minute they were talking over coffee, and the next she was pinned under his talented mouth, being eaten until — what had he said? She kept begging for more.

Yeah, that summed it up.

She caught his jaw and dragged him upward, on fire by the hard muscle of his body rubbing against her bare, overly sensitive skin. Hovering over her, he looked down into her eyes.

She ran her thumb over his lips, wet with her juices. "Kiss me," she whispered.

An animalistic groan left him, and he plastered his mouth over hers, sharing her flavors and that of the man himself. Coffee, toothpaste. Wheeler.

She went for his waistband a second time, and again, he stopped her. Pinning her wrists to the bed, he breathed heavily for a second.

"It's been a long time for me, honey. I don't want to embarrass myself."

"Let me take off your clothes at least."

"One touch and I'll blow."

"How about two?" She squirmed, and he released her, rolling onto the mattress and giving her a beautiful view of the dips and swells of his shoulders, chest and abs.

"Mm." She pressed a kiss to his pec, moving down to his taut nipple. When she circled it with her tongue, he cupped her head to him and let out a moan.

Encouraged by this, she continued to explore, tasting every square inch of his perfect body. Then she climbed off the bed and gripped his boot. One pull and it was off.

"Wish you could do that with the cast," he rumbled, eyes burning with intensity.

"I got other tricks."

"Oh?" He arched a brow.

She went for his jeans, and it didn't take much to get them off, though she might have torn one of the worn spots wider. Neither cared as she removed his boxers so his hard, long cock sprang free.

He watched her closely, and she had a hard time containing her reaction.

"I've never wanted any man this much in my life," she whispered through dry lips.

A smile eased across his rugged features, and he gripped his shaft at the base, standing it up.

"If you'll do the honors, honey, condoms are in the drawer."

"And here I thought only your foot was broken."

He shot her a crooked grin as she leaned to the side to pull open the drawer. At first, she wasn't sure if she'd find a condom at all—underneath the knife was a firearm and a cache of bullets came sliding forward. Normal cowboy nightstand, as far as she could see, especially the tinderbox and a fat candle that could be set atop the nightstand in the event of a power outage.

She peered into the drawer and spotted a couple lone condoms in the corner. Snagging both, she offered him a flirty smile.

"Am I gettin' lucky twice then?" he drawled.

"If you do a good enough job the first time."

He chuckled. "Honey, by the time I'm finished with you, the neighbors will need a cigarette, and they're four miles off."

"I'll be the judge." Though by looking at the man stretched out on the bed, she was pretty damn impressed. And that mouth of his could do more than give directions about his horse or fall into a grim line if she did things her own way.

As she ripped open the packet, it hit her that they hadn't known each other long at all. Hours, really. She had never been a one-night stand kind of girl, but this didn't feel that way. Besides, her body was humming with need each time she glanced at his impressive erection, and she had no reason to back out. This would not be something she regretted.

He reached for the condom and watched her face as he fit it over his swollen head and stroked it downward over his length. A warm shiver of heat ran through her body. She moved upward to lie next to him. Her hair fell over her shoulder and teased his too.

"C'mere," he growled, cupping her nape and pulling her close. The initial brush of his lips was hard but he demanded she open to him with a flick of his tongue. When she did, he took total control of the kiss, drawing her up to straddle him as he devoured her lips and tongue and made her forget her own name.

Passion rose inside of her, something she hadn't known before now. But why was it just now happening with a stranger, a man she knew little about, when she'd had months to get close to Jason?

Sometimes a horse just isn't the right match for the rider, no matter how much you try.

Her daddy's words flooded her mind, but the minute Wheeler cradled her breasts in his rough palms, her focus was only on him. All thoughts and memories receded to the back of her brain as she gave herself up to his exquisite touch.

He kneaded her breasts lightly while he kissed her, and each time he swiped a thumb across one of her nipples, she cried out. Every noise gaining in strength until she was rising and falling into his touch.

He let go of her breasts and moved his hands down over her middle to land on her hips. He curled his fingers close to her hipbones and guided her up— and down over his cock.

The pressure of him stretching her tight inner walls had her crying out. He issued a harsh groan. When he broke the kiss, he looked into her eyes. "Look at me."

She did, and he slid her body down until he was filling her to the hilt.

"Oh God," she panted.

"Damn." A tendon in the crease of his jaw worked in and out, and his eyes were dark. "You're so fucking warm, honey."

She pushed up on her knees, withdrawing on him. The flicker of pleasure in his eyes was something she wanted to put there again. She slid down.

"Hell. Easy on me, cowgirl."

She flashed a grin and began to move. At first she moved because it felt good and she wanted to share that with him too, but after half a dozen strokes, she hung forward, too engrossed in anything but the wicked sensation of a big cock inside her.

Then he kissed her, and she had her first orgasm around him.

* * * * *

The clench and release of Aria's pussy around his length had him gritting back his own explosion. He gripped her hips and drove her faster as liquid heat enveloped him. Her tongue grew slack against his, and he continued to kiss her gently, rolling her over while still buried balls deep in her.

She hitched her thighs high on his hips and spiraled her arms around his neck, clinging to him as he forced pulse after pulse from her tight pussy and he shoved his own orgasm back.

Need blasted over him, though, and it was all he could do to go slowly and give her the time to build once more. Besides, he wasn't so sure he'd get that second chance, and he was making the most of the first.

Staring down at her beautiful face—eyes wide and glittering with pleasure and her cheeks flushed pink—was his only thought at this very moment.

She was gorgeous. Smart, sassy and skilled. All the things he never believed he could find in a woman all at once.

But she was also a celebrity on the run from a fiancé that she could very well patch things up with.

Firmly nudging the thought from his mind, he braced himself on his elbows and cradled her jaw. Bringing her lips back to his, he pushed his cock deep. She cried out, angling up to meet his thrust.

And another.

Soon they were breathing heavily and her fingers dug into his back. Every withdrawal of his shaft through her tight walls raised a growl to his lips, and she cried out in return. Digging his foot in this way made it ache, but he didn't give a damn. All that mattered was reaching that explosive end and taking Aria with him for the ride.

Sweat snaked down his neck, and she wore a damp sheen across her throat and the tops of her breasts too. He moved in for another kiss, and their mouths clashed with a brand new level of heat.

He lost himself, hips pumping, gripping her to him. When she clamped down on him and bit into his lower lip, he let out a moan and shot forward to the finish line.

Extreme pressure rose up from his core and hit him full force. He threw his head back on a yell of ecstasy, lashing her body to his and finding her lips in the rush of bliss and emotions that flooded in.

"Aria…" Her name dropped from his tongue like the sweetest honey.

She thumped him on the shoulder with a final cry, twitching in his hold. "Wheeler."

Long seconds passed while he gathered his wits, and then he withdrew from her and got up to use the bathroom. A second later he returned and crawled into bed with her.

She popped her head off the pillow, eyes wide. "You didn't use your crutches."

"Shit, I forgot. Guess it serves as a walking cast too."

"No way. You can't bear weight on it till the doctor tells you to. Didn't it hurt?"

He shrugged and gathered her close, tucking her head beneath his chin. Hell, did she have to fit here just right? Like a well-made saddle that conformed to him in all the right places.

He dragged in a deep breath of their sex-scented air, and some of her hair tickled his nose. "You used my shampoo."

"It was all you had in the shower. Was that okay?"

He rumbled without being able to stop it. "I like it," he said quietly.

She practically wiggled with energy in his arms.

"Clearly you're not one of those women who nods off after sex," he said.

She giggled. "That's men you're thinking of."

"Hmm."

Bringing her palm up the swell of his chest, she said, "That really just happened, didn't it?"

When he nodded, her hair caught on the scruff of his jaw. His throat was a little tight on any words he could think to say. Yeah, that had happened, and it would live forever in his mind. Not only as the best sex he'd ever experienced but the stirring in his chest was altogether new to him.

Don't get attached. She can't run forever.

But I can keep her safe until she's ready. And plenty satisfied too.

It wouldn't be enough, and he knew it. But he was willing to suffer any heart pangs when she finally left him. Right now, he'd enjoy every minute of her silky, nude body wrapped around his.

"Wheeler?"

He opened his eyes and shifted to peer down at her. Those warm brown eyes of hers could slay him with a single look. Hell, he was already in trouble. Was this how King had felt with Bellarose?

What was the damn chance that Wheeler would end up with a woman from the TV show the way his friend had? When he thought of Aria, though, it wasn't the actor he saw but the woman with a tenderness for horses and a way of bullying Wheeler into doing what was best for him, like putting his foot up.

She went on talking. "Is it terrible that I didn't think about the man who wanted to marry me once during what we just did?"

"Christ, I hope you didn't."

"I don't mean that. I was a thousand percent focused on you. It's just that… If I really loved him, I wouldn't have let you start things by kissing me. Then I wouldn't have encouraged you."

"You begged me." He earned a sharp look from her before she went on.

"It's just that…" She trailed off.

"Look, honey." He bracketed her face with his hands, which were so large in comparison to her delicate features. "You can't beat yourself up over him. There were too many questions or you would be married right now. It didn't have to do with you not planning the wedding and him springing it on you. Because if you seriously, deep down wanted to marry him, it wouldn't have mattered one bit where, how or when it happened."

Her eyes softened under his gaze. "You're right," she said softly.

"So that's the last time you question yourself. You're a good woman, Aria. Just because you didn't want to marry that action flick guy with the millions in the bank and a house with a pool—"

"Two pools. He has one indoors and out."

He huffed out a breath. "And here I was just stereotyping. But either way, honey… you don't have to apologize for not wanting those things for yourself. Now, if he had a hot tub and you passed that by... then I'd say you'd better find yourself a shrink."

A laugh escaped her, and she swatted him in the ear. "You're horrible."

He arched a brow and gave her a wicked smile. "Wanna find out just how horrible?"

Her teeth closed on her plump lower lip. She nodded and drew his hand to her breast. Instantly, her nipple crested under his touch. Not willing to wait another second, he claimed her lips.

After long minutes, she broke their kiss. "How far is it to town?"

"Twenty minutes or so." He found her soaking center and pushed two fingers inside her.

She cried out, neck arched and eyes pinched shut. He was already fully hard and ready to sink between her rounded thighs. Suddenly, he caught on to what she was asking.

"Guess I'd better get ready to make a supply run. You like this brand or do you favor the ribbed for your pleasure?"

Wrapping her arms around him and pulling him down atop her, she shot him a smile that was like a ray of light slanting through his life. "These are just fine. Take me, cowboy."

He didn't need to be asked twice. He just hoped this flash of light in his universe wasn't like a comet, quickly passing through just once in his lifetime.

Chapter Six

The nights here in Washington weren't much different from Montana. Cool and crisp with a fresh mountain wind blowing the ends of her hair back over her shoulders. Aria stood at the railing on the front porch and stared into the darkness.

A step sounded behind her, and she turned to see Wheeler coming through the door, crutches leading the way. When he met her gaze, she waited to feel the hit of remorse for sleeping with him. He was a stranger, after all.

But it didn't come, and she was relieved to not have to think on her actions. What they'd shared was a fun time, a blowing off of steam, and they both needed it. No harm was done, so she wasn't going to fixate on the stolen moments. Besides all that, he was a great listener, and she'd needed that ear.

"Couldn't sleep?" Her voice was caught up in the breeze.

"Felt uneasy. Thought I'd check my stock."

Her brows went up in surprise. "Gusto was fine when I put him to bed."

"Yeah, but a cowboy's got a sixth sense."

No arguing with that—she'd witnessed it herself more than once on her family's ranch.

"I'll come with you."

In silence, they made their way across the darkened yard to the barn. Walking next to him felt strangely brand new, and there was an awareness between them that came from exploring each other's bodies thoroughly, not only twice but several more times, using mouths and hands to pleasure when the condoms ran out.

They reached the barn, and he flipped on a light. She squinted toward Gusto's stall. From here, she couldn't tell if Wheeler was right about something being off, but she moved forward with the intention to find out.

"Damn, I hate not being able to do for my horse. Do you mind leading him out for me to look at?" Frustration backlit Wheeler's words.

"I got it."

She approached the door and assessed the horse in the dim light of a couple bare bulbs in the center of the barn. She was surprised there was electricity down here at all—most older outbuildings didn't have such luxuries.

The horse didn't make a sound as she reached past the door to stroke its nose. Or when she opened the door and got a rope around him to draw him into the center of the space.

"Shit. Look at that leg. Swelling again." Wheeler's agitation rubbed off on the horse, and he shifted from foot to foot but found it hurt too much and he lifted it.

"Crap. Do you think he strained it again somehow while out in the paddock?"

"Don't know."

"Should I call the vet?"

"Let's see if we can get it to come down before we call. Do you mind helping me ice it again?"

"Of course not. I'll go back to the house and get the ice." Earlier the previous day, Wheeler had shown her a small freezer unit on the mud porch with enough bags of ice to keep them going for a while. She ran the distance, not worried about the darkness or uneven ground. Country girls were sure-footed, and she was confident.

When she returned with the bag, she dropped it onto the floor to break it up inside the bag.

"Got your knife on you?" she asked Wheeler.

He produced one from his pocket and she slit the bag open, dumping a generous amount into the bucket. Then she carried it outside and found the water hose. She filled the bucket deep enough to envelope the horse's injured leg and hauled the heavy bucket back inside.

Wheeler looked about to spit nails. "I should have done something more."

"Not sure what that would have been. We followed the vet's instructions to the T and he said just hours ago that it was doing well." Concern wrinkled her brow as she eased the horse to the bucket and urged it to place its hoof down into the icy water. No horse liked this unless it was a deadly hot day, but it was for its own good.

"C'mon, boy," she crooned, stroking his mane.

Slowly, the horse relaxed enough to lower its hoof to the ice water.

Balancing on his one crutch, Wheeler bent to examine it. "Skin isn't broken. Can't be infection."

"No, unless it's coming up from the hoof but that's impossible. The vet would have said."

"Maybe just overuse for the day," Wheeler grumbled.

As Gusto stood in the ice bath, she got the brush to go over his coat and soothe him further.

"He likes that." Wheeler's voice was gritty.

She smiled. "I used to like my momma brushing my hair when I was a little girl. I've seen all animals act the same. Have you ever forked a pig?"

"Only for Christmas dinner."

She grinned. "I had a few pigs as pets over the years, and our vet told us that to calm them down in order to give them a shot or something, to run a fork over their hide. It's like an intense massage is to a human, by my guess, and they love it."

"You surprise me, Aria."

She looked up. "Why?"

"All the things you do and say make you into a perfect woman. Or at least in my eyes."

Shock jerked at her heartstrings.

"And just when I start wondering if I'm amplifying it all in my head, blowing you up into something more, you say something else that makes me know that you really are the most amazing woman I've ever met."

She stared at him, words fled from her lips. How to respond to such a sweet and heartfelt compliment?

She couldn't.

Reaching out, she took his hand, meshing their fingers for a moment as she looked into his eyes.

After a second, he pulled away. "Maybe my brain got addled after that fall," he mumbled.

They remained together for a good half hour, icing the horse's leg. When it was time for it to come out of the bucket, Gusto allowed her to pull the leg up without resistance. She followed the lines of tendon down the leg.

"Does it seem less swollen to you?" she asked Wheeler.

"A bit. Let's give him an hour off, and I'll come down and do it again."

She arched a brow. "Not without my help. We're in this for the night, cowboy."

* * * * *

115

Aria's shoulders drooped, and she slumped down farther in her chair. Her food was uneaten, and sometime during the night she'd gathered her hair up in a leather thong she'd found somewhere and knotted it off her face. The look was devastating on him—he couldn't stop looking at her.

He had a feeling he was a little more than infatuated. Smitten, maybe. But they'd only spent a few days together—and a steamy night tumbling in each other's arms too—and he couldn't help but feel this entire moment in his life was just that. A heartbeat, a blip in the mundane of his world.

She'd return to her life and how could he add up to more? A wrangler like him, laid up with a busted foot... He had no money to speak of, hardly had time to take care of himself between his work with King and the small chores he managed to do around his own place.

He didn't have time for a woman, anyway. Wooin', old-fashioned courtin', datin' all required time and money, both of which he was short on.

Well, he had the time right now, but the crutches couldn't add to his appeal.

"Why don't you take the bed?" he suggested. "Get some rest."

She looked up, but he saw something more in her gaze, and she worried her lip with her teeth.

"What is it?" he asked gently.

"I have to go back, don't I?"

116

His heart twisted in his chest. Studying her, he asked, "Don't you want to?"

A second passed before she gave a nod. Looking down at her plate of eggs, she nodded a second time. "Of course I do. It's a great job, and I'm so lucky that I have it. So many people would kill to do what I do."

She sounded far from convinced or happy about it.

"I'll go back to the set this afternoon."

Fuck. So soon. It really was a blip in time, wasn't it? One heartbeat out of millions he'd live in his life.

Only this was one he'd remember more than the rest.

"I can drive you down if you want." His offer held only resignation.

"Yes. But first..." Her eyes burned into him, leaving him scorched and shell-shocked. How, in a couple days, had she managed to become such a huge part of his existence?

He ached to reach out to her. "But first what?"

"I'd like to visit Bellarose. Would you take me up there?"

"Won't she be on set today?" he asked.

"Isn't this Wednesday?"

He nodded.

"It's her day off."

"All right then." He lay his hand flat on the table. "We'll go after we get cleaned up. Eat your eggs, honey."

A smile ghosted across her face, so small and swift, vanishing quickly. "Only if you promise to prop your foot while I'm in the shower."

How was he going to get through the rest of these long, dull days of his recovery without the vibrant woman seated across from him? He'd even miss her ordering him around.

* * * * *

"This place is beautiful." Aria stared at King Yates' ranch, known as Blackwater. From the sign they'd driven under to the miles of pristine fencing, she was impressed with the entire operation.

"Yeah, it's not bad to look." Wheeler's dry tone brought a smile to her lips. He took a left turn and they rolled up in front of a modest cabin.

She wrung her hands. "Suddenly, I'm nervous."

"Well, if I was coming back from the dead and showing up on Bellarose and King's doorstep, I'd feel the same." He parked the truck and shot her a look.

"I'm hardly coming back from the dead. Do you have to tease me on top of all the emotional discomfort I'm already in?" Her words were softened by her playful sidelong look.

"I'm not the one on the run." The crooked smile tormenting her insides was something she wouldn't mind seeing more of. Back in the kitchen, she had made the final choice to return to the set. Most of the night while watching over the horse, she'd had plenty of time to face her demons. In the end, she'd decided to return sooner than she originally wanted because she could still hear her daddy's voice echoing in her head from their earlier conversation.

He hadn't agreed with the way she was handling things but had relayed his trust in her. Being raised by the man who didn't give trust lightly, Aria knew that was code for her to think on what she was doing. As a child, if these words were spoken to her, it always gave her pause. More than once she'd considered some rash mistake before making it and veered the other direction.

Wheeler got out of the truck and pulled down his crutches. As he made his way around the rear, Aria stared at the cabin. Well, this was her first step in taking more control of her life.

She wasn't friends with Bellarose but she wanted to be, so she would make an overture starting right now.

She waited for Wheeler to catch up to her and together, they headed to the cabin. A high-pitched yipping bark brought her attention around just as a herd dog, speckled with one blue eye and one brown, came barreling around the corner of a huge barn.

As it launched itself at Wheeler, he swung his injured foot back to protect it. What was a large and energetic pup launched itself at the man.

"Awww, did ya miss, me, boy? He reached down to scratch its ears." Glancing away from the dog to Aria's face, he said, "This here's Jack."

At his name, the dog wagged his tail wildly.

Aria reached out to let him sniff her fingers. When she was cleared as no threat, she patted the shepherd's head. "Hey, boy. You're pretty nice, aren't ya?"

When she was finished fussing over the dog, she looked up to find Wheeler staring at her.

"Ready?" he asked.

She drew a deep breath. "Yes."

As they approached the house, the pup circled them and Wheeler scolded him to keep away from his crutches. No sooner had they neared the porch steps than the door opened and Bellarose stepped out.

Her jaw dropped at the sight of Aria, and she rushed forward. "Oh my God! You're safe!"

Aria couldn't have felt lower than she did at this moment, knowing the worry she had caused everyone. She'd stupidly believed that since she was a new actor to the show, she was less important. But that obviously wasn't the case, if Bellarose's tears were anything to go by.

"I'm fine, and I'm so sorry for worrying you."

Bellarose took her by the shoulders and gave her a little shake before pulling her in for an embrace. Aria was an only child, and this was as close as she'd ever come to feeling like someone's little sister.

The woman Aria looked up to and was more than shy around jerked her head to the side, piercing Wheeler in her gaze. She planted a hand on her hip. "Tell me that you don't have something to do with this."

"All I did was find her in my barn."

"Barn? When?" She looked between them.

"Maybe we should sit down," he suggested.

"Oh dear. Yes, we should. How is your foot?" She opened the door and ushered them both inside. When the puppy tried to follow as well, she told him to lie down and wait for King. They went inside, leaving the puppy on the porch wagging its tail.

Once she'd led them to the living room, she looked at Aria. "I was so worried. We all are."

"I know. I'm very sorry that I took off. It was a hasty decision and one I regret." She glanced at Wheeler. *But I don't regret it the way I probably should.* "When Jason showed up with that ring and the dress and flowers… I just flipped. I didn't even think about what I'd done until I was in Wheeler's barn and curled up in the stall crying."

Bellarose pressed her fingers to her lips and shook her head. "They called off the search—I heard that much—but I didn't know why till now. You called into the sheriff's office."

Wheeler nodded.

Aria sat next to him on a leather sofa and felt herself looking to him for support. Which was insane,

121

because they were new friends and she shouldn't be relying on him quite this much so soon.

Their circumstances had bound them quickly, though. She needed him, he needed her. Then the intimacy of the previous night...

She tried not to give anything away to Bellarose, but the woman was already looking between them.

"Wheeler was kind enough to let me stay at his place while I collected myself. And I helped him with the chores and his horse that's injured."

"The horse is improved King said," Bellarose said.

"Took a bad turn last night with his leg swelling, but we caught it in time and Aria spent all night icing it. This morning it looks much better."

"I'm glad to hear that then. But... Wheeler, you were here yesterday. King was at your place too. And Aria was hiding out with you the entire time?"

"That was by my request," Aria spoke up, taking the blame on herself. "I didn't want to say where I was, bring the media down on Wheeler." When she met his stare, he gave a short nod, and she reached out and brushed her fingers over his knuckles.

An action that was not lost on Bellarose.

The dog yipped again outside. "That'll be King." A minute later, his heavy boot steps rang on the wooden floors of the cabin. When he entered the room, he stopped dead.

With his stare on Wheeler, he said, "I take it this is Aria."

"Yes, isn't it wonderful she's safe? And with Wheeler the whole time," Bellarose spoke up.

King cocked a brow. "Care to join me on the porch for a beer?"

Wheeler was on his crutches immediately and stumping after the man, leaving Aria alone with Bellarose.

"I feel terrible."

Bellarose reached out and squeezed her hand. "Why don't we have some tea? C'mon."

They went into the kitchen, which was homey with modern touches like new granite counters and stainless appliances. "You know, I had a feeling you had landed on your feet and nothing bad had happened to you." Bellarose directed a lock of red hair behind her ear as she lit the burner under the teapot.

Aria slid onto a barstool and folded her hands on the countertop. "I have no excuses except to say I'm new to this life and I freaked."

"Jason Lee didn't stick around long. He was pretty broken up, I hear."

Aria rubbed a hand over her eyes. "I need to speak with him. I still haven't figured out what to say."

"I'm pretty certain he knows you don't want to marry him." Amusement tinged her tone and she smiled gently at Aria.

Funny how they'd spoken little to each other over the course of filming, but now that she was seated in Bellarose's kitchen, Aria couldn't figure out why she'd been shy around her. She was very intuitive and kind about the situation.

"I'm sure I'm on every tabloid and magazine in the free world right now."

"Pretty much, yeah. But mostly because nobody knows what happened to you. How on earth did you end up with Wheeler? And what is going on between you?" Bellarose got down two mugs from a shelf and added teabags to each.

Aria jolted. "What do you mean what is going on between us? Nothing."

"Hmm. I've never seen Wheeler look at a woman the way I just saw him look at you. How long have you known each other?"

"You... you think that I'd met Wheeler before and he's the reason I didn't want to marry Jason?" She shook her head. "I took off running and ended up at his place. It was dark and I didn't want to be met on the porch with a shotgun, so I slipped into his barn and fell asleep, thinking to leave first thing. But then he came to the barn and found me."

"This sounds like something the writers would come up with for *Redemption Falls*." Bellarose chuckled.

"Ugh, it does, doesn't it? It's worse than the stepbrother storyline for sure, and Wheeler made fun of that."

She pondered Bellarose's revelation that she'd never seen Wheeler look at a woman like he'd looked at Aria. Warmth spread over her at the mere thought, and she hoped she hid it away well enough. She was far from ready to discuss anything concerning Wheeler. Not that anything was going on—they were friends.

Who'd slept together.

Several times.

But it had only been one night.

Who was she kidding? If she stayed with him a second, third, or more, she'd land in his bed every single time.

"Bellarose, you've been in the industry longer than I have. I appreciate your opinion or any advice you can offer me on how to get myself out of this awful mess. With the running away, with Jason, and then not telling people where I was right away…"

"And with Wheeler?"

Long seconds passed.

"You don't need to explain to me if you don't want. But I know Wheeler and I'm a willing listener if you need to get anything off your chest." Bellarose rescued the kettle from the flames and poured their mugs.

Aria took another minute to gather her thoughts. "No," she said slowly. "Oddly, I know exactly where I stand with Wheeler."

"And that is?"

"We're friends, I think. Not sure how it happened so fast, but I guess it was being thrown into a tough situation and helping each other out. But..."

"Go on." She added sugar to her tea.

Aria picked up her spoon and stirred the hot drink. "I haven't made decisions for myself for a long time. Like... years. I landed this acting role and never tried for it. It was handed to me—I didn't choose it. I don't know if I'm making sense. But when faced with a wedding and a man I didn't love... Well, I finally snapped and made a rash decision based on emotions. I ran. But it was a choice of my own for once, and I made another when I begged Wheeler not to tell anybody of my whereabouts." She gave a low laugh. "He didn't even know who I was at first sight. It was refreshing not to be recognized, I'll say."

Bellarose laughed. "I believe it. I'm married to a man who didn't even know me at all."

They shared a chuckle and sipped their tea. After a moment, Bellarose lowered her mug and eyed Aria.

"What is your next step?"

"I'm going back. Today." She might have sounded a bit too forceful.

126

"Wheeler is a grumpy bear with his broken foot, isn't he? King said he'd be as much."

"No, it isn't Wheeler. He's... he's good." She felt heat rising into her cheeks and buried her nose in the mug, but not before Bellarose shot her a knowing look.

"He's one of the best cattle handlers this side of the Mississippi. He's been asked to go all over, but he refuses and stays right here helping King."

Aria looked up in surprise. Something had nagged at her about Wheeler from the start. "You don't think he's... stuck, do you?"

"Stuck?"

"Like, frozen in place and can't make choices to move forward with his life. He says he never thought much about expanding his own ranch, but I wondered if that might be fear guiding him."

She considered it for a minute. "King would be the better one to answer that question. They've known each other most of their lives. But no, I think it's more the work that Wheeler loves. Being outdoors, going to bed exhausted but knowing you did your duty that day. I think to him, it doesn't matter who owns the stock."

"Makes sense. I just wondered if..."

"If?"

She met Bellarose's stare head on. "If I'm not the only person who can't make decisions. Do you believe that people run into your path in life for a reason? To show you something you're doing wrong or right or even that you need a different path entirely?"

Bellarose nodded. "I do. You know, shortly after I signed the contract for *Redemption Falls*, I was offered another job, a bigger one, for more money. But I had a feeling about this one and if I'm honest with myself, it went deeper than me getting the Emmy for it last season."

Aria smiled. It was nice to talk to someone like-minded who didn't consider her a raving lunatic for suggesting that she might have landed in Wheeler's barn for a reason. She couldn't help but think he needed her and she needed him just as much in that moment of their lives. Two planets finding the same orbit.

But it was time for her to fix her path.

Maybe she could continue seeing Wheeler sometimes. Come up and check on Gusto and the girls.

And make sure Wheeler was obeying doctor's orders about his foot.

"If I hadn't stayed on the show, I never would have met King." Bellarose's smile was angelic as she talked about her husband, and Aria knew her love reached deeper than anyone could ever know.

"So if I hadn't run away from Jason Lee..."

They shared another laugh, this one sad. Aria said, "Oh, poor Jason. I have to call him tonight. I can't let more time pass."

Bellarose patted her hand. "You know who to come talk to if you need a sympathetic ear."

"Thank you. I haven't had a friend here, and I realized it's because I kept to myself. But I'd like to change that, if you don't mind being my first friend."

Bellarose's eyes gleamed and she hopped off the stool to come put her arms around Aria. She hugged her back, happy to have someone for good old-fashioned girl talk.

* * * * *

"All right. What are you doing with her?" King got right to the point.

"Wow, that's a new record. I don't think your ass even hit that seat before the words flew out of your mouth." Wheeler took longer to sit, lowering himself with one foot jutting out in front of him.

"You didn't say a damn word yesterday when I was telling you how worried my wife was about Aria."

"No, and I'm sorry for it. She asked me not to tell."

"And again, I'll ask what you're doing with her."

"Nothin'. I gave her a place to hide out a coupla days, and she helped with chores and did some things around the house too."

King set the beer cap against the arm of the chair, which was scarred from doing that very thing, and popped the top off. "Is that why you can't keep your eyes off her?"

Wheeler groaned. "That's such a common thing to say. That a red-blooded man can't keep his eyes off a beautiful woman."

King snorted and brought the bottle to his lips. "Well, it's true. I've never seen you look at someone like that before is all."

Because he hadn't. But he wasn't about to admit to his buddy that he was smitten with her. He turned the topic to the horses and how the training had been going since he broke his foot. King filled him in on all the idiosyncrasies of running short-handed, and they discussed the cattle and how Schmitty and King would need to move them alone to greener pastures soon.

"Man, I wish I could ride. Don't see why I can't just let the foot dangle when I ride." Wheeler swigged his beer.

"You gonna rope your crutches onto the saddle too? It's only six weeks, Wheeler. Give yourself the time to heal."

"Maybe I can use the ATV. At least feed and check the herd. Be of some damn use."

King contemplated him. "Not a bad idea. Let me think on it. I don't want you to have a setback because you're working too soon."

"If you ever get in this position, and I hope you don't, you'll know how damn hard it is."

"Not as hard with a pretty brunette around, though."

With a shake of his head, he said, "You never let up, do you? She's been a damn good help with Gusto. Knew just what to do for his leg, and without her, I would have struggled a lot more."

"That's how you knew she's a Montana girl." King's statement told Wheeler he'd just put two and two together.

"Apologized already, didn't I? Stop sounding like a whiny little brother who didn't know there were cookies till they were all gone."

King huffed a laugh and eyed him. "So she's a cookie. And I'd be the big brother."

"Dude, shut up." Wheeler grinned and took a sip. Thank God nothing more was said, because the ladies came outside then, pushing through the screen door. Wheeler started to get up, driven by the manners his momma had bred in him, and King was already up and ushering his wife to his seat.

"Can I have your beer too?" she asked.

"Darlin', you can have anything you want." He smiled into her eyes and she took his beer and handed him a mug of tea.

A month ago, Wheeler might have wondered at this type of exchange, but somehow, Aria had changed his thinking.

"Don't get up." She settled a hand on his shoulder and that one small touch reached deep inside him and heated his chest.

He plunked back into the seat and she went to lean against the railing and look out over the ranch.

God, he was out of his league. No way would he have a chance at more with a woman like Aria. She belonged on a place like this, was practically ranch royalty and to top it all off, everybody knew her as a rising star. What did he have to offer? A ride in his decade-old truck with spots of rust and dinner at the local mom and pop joint for today's special?

She hitched a boot onto the bottom rail and leaned forward, giving him a perfect view of her round ass.

He buried his focus in polishing off his beer. Sweetest thing he'd have were his memories, and those would have to last him a long time.

Memories of that luscious ass in his palms, dragging her down and onto his cock. Of her lips... and dammit, her eyes as she splintered apart for him with a throaty cry of passion.

Hell.

Two of King's top horses were housed together to keep each other company, and just then they came into sight, running the line of fence in a game of chase.

Aria straightened, and Wheeler couldn't sit there another second. He got up and drifted to the railing to stand next to her. Even to smell her and feel the warmth coming off her skin would have to do.

"They're beautiful," she said. "I've missed this so much."

He watched her face a moment, heart doing little tricks in his chest. It was on the tip of his tongue to say he'd miss *her* so much, but he bit back the words. Sensing someone watching him, he tossed a look over his shoulder. Sure enough, King and Bellarose were staring.

Tugging his hat low, he faced forward again. "Maybe after the filming, you should go back to Montana for a visit," he suggested.

Her gaze snapped to him. "Maybe I could. You'd love—" She broke off and pinched her lips together, watching the horses again.

He didn't know what she was about to say, but it sounded like it could be that he'd love it there.

Dwelling on it would do him no good, and he had to shake off any notion of there being more between them. He had a life to live, and so did she. In fact, she needed to get back to the set.

As if she realized this too, she turned to him. "I think it's time."

He nodded and together they faced King and Bellarose. "Thanks for the refreshments and talk. We're gonna get on the road."

"I'm so glad you came to me, Aria. I'll see you tomorrow on set." Bellarose came forward to grip Aria's hands. The women embraced.

"Ah shucks. See ya soon, King." Wheeler reached up to pound his buddy on the back, and the women broke apart to laugh at them.

"Stay off that foot. Want me to come down and check the horse in a while?"

Wheeler gave a shake of his head. "I got it, but thanks."

As they made their way back to Wheeler's truck, silence fell over them.

She got into the passenger's seat, and he worked his way to the driver's side and tossed the crutches in the back. When he closed the door, quiet surrounded them, closed them in.

She stared down at her hands in her lap.

"I sense a weight on you, Aria. Going back will mean facing a lot of things, but you're strong."

She nodded. "Thank you."

"There might be something that could lighten your spirits."

She turned her brown eyes on him, sending sparks shooting through his system, especially with what he was about to tell her.

"This morning when I was rooting around in the truck, I found something."

"What's that?"

He slanted a crooked grin at her before leaning across her thighs and popping the glove compartment. There, resting on top of a pile of paperwork for the truck, was a single foil packet.

Her sharp little intake of air made his smile spread. He plucked up the condom and held it out to her. "Whattaya say, honey?"

"Can't let it go to waste." She ran her tongue over her lips in suggestion. "Start the truck, Wheeler. We can't do it in Bellarose and King's driveway."

"You don't need to ask me twice." He twisted the key, heart pumping with excitement that he'd have one more stolen moment with this amazing woman.

Chapter Seven

Wheeler stepped out of the truck and instead of grabbing the crutches, he reached behind the seat and pulled out a blanket roll. His cock was already fully hard, and he'd barely made it onto a back road to stop the truck and reach for Aria.

Her reaction to him finding that condom had given him one hell of an ego boost too. She slid out of the truck and slammed the door. When she rounded the back, their gazes collided.

He felt those sparks all the way to the tips of his toes. Holding out the blanket, he rumbled, "Will you do the honors?"

With a tempting grin, she took the blanket, walked a little ways off and unfurled it. He followed as quickly as he could with one crutch.

The spot he'd chosen was relatively flat with a small clearing in the pines that provided a nice view of the mountain. The slate blue peak would ordinarily claim his attention on a good day of riding, but nothing could make him look away from the beautiful woman facing him.

She stepped up close and reached for her shirt buttons.

His mouth dried out as he watched her nimble fingers work down the line until a sliver of tanned skin was revealed. With a flick of her finger, she twitched the cotton aside. "You want me, cowboy?"

"Damn right I do." He practically growled out the words and let his crutch fall. Stepping up to her, he slipped his hands into the open edges of her top, clasping warm, silken skin that rippled with goosebumps the moment he laid hands on her.

Bracing her palms on his chest, she moved to stand between his legs. She looked up into his eyes and then slowly pulled off his hat. "You know, if a man takes off his hat to kiss a woman, he's a keeper."

His lips quirked up. "That so?"

"Yes."

"What does it mean when she takes his hat off before he can get to it?"

Her brown eyes burned with desire. "It means she wants him bad."

He couldn't restrain his growl this time and claimed her lips. A dark need gripped him as he plunged his tongue into her mouth, taking every small cry she'd give up to him — demanding more.

She circled his neck with her arms, pulling him down. He caught her against him, and supporting her weight, swept her off her feet and laid her on the blanket, buckling at the knees to follow her down.

Her thighs parted automatically for him, and he pressed his erection into the heat between her legs. "I'm about to burst my zipper for you, honey."

"Can't have that." She went for his fly, and he reached beneath her to pop the clasp of her bra. The instant her nipples were freed, he bent to take one in his mouth and continued to fumble off her clothes.

When he eased his hand inside her panties, a full-body shudder rolled over her, and he felt her tense against his hand.

"Fuck, you're slicker than the slope to hell. Give me your mouth." He crushed his lips over hers and sank one finger into her tight sheath. Liquid heat enveloped his hand and thundered through the rest of him.

She'd managed to get his belt loosened and the button of his jeans free, but the instant he touched her, she'd focused on the pleasure he was giving her.

Just the way he wanted it—with Aria desperate and needy.

Maybe then she'll come back for more.

Unlikely, but a cowboy could dream.

He kissed her senseless, distracting her from the fact he was stripping her clothes off. With boots, socks, jeans and panties off, and her top and bra only partially covering her, he gave her a wicked smile before lowering himself in a slow, easy glide down to her pussy.

She was ripe as a peach, soaking wet and ready for his tongue. Flattening it over her clit, he teased at her opening with his fingers.

Clapping her hands around his ears, she threw her head back. "Yes, Wheeler!"

Encouraged by her raspy cry, he buried two fingers deep into her pussy and lapped her clit. Need clutched at his balls at her flavors on his tongue and the way she flooded his fingers with more juices. Glancing up the length of her body, he watched her eyes open wide and then her lids droop with each move of his fingers.

He pulled her clit between his lips and swirled his tongue across the bundle of nerves. She sucked in a gasp and plastered her hands over his shoulders, hips moving to get closer to his mouth.

Fuck, she was gorgeous, desirable and did she have to be so damn perfect? Because now he was ruined for any other woman. Didn't matter who came along after Aria—it wouldn't *be* Aria, and he couldn't see anything but her.

Her hair tumbled across the blanket, and the tiny point of her chin strained toward the sky as he sucked on her nubbin and fingered her pussy. A rough groan left him, which she echoed with a feminine moan of her own.

With a final plunge into her pussy, he applied pressure to her inner wall. A pulsation met his fingertips, and he knew he'd found her G-spot. With slow precision, he massaged it. Lightly, a fleeting touch. Then pressing harder and dragging a cry from her.

"Wh..." Her mouth opened on a silent cry that seemed to go on for long minutes. "Wheeler. Please."

She wanted to come, and hell if he wanted to hold her back.

He doubled his efforts, drawing on her clit with lips and tongue and massaging her G-spot in a steady rhythm that would send her shooting over the edge fast and hard.

Too late he realized he should drag out this moment. It was unlikely he'd get another—he was out of condoms and she was going back to her life. But when the first contraction of her inner walls gripped his fingers and a loud cry ripped through the air, he couldn't be sorry anymore.

He leaned upward to mouth her clit as he fucked her hard and fast. His gaze centered on her beautiful face as she came apart for him, rocking her hips over and over and finally collapsing to the blanket, trembling.

She lifted her shaking hands to his jaw and looked into his eyes. "You're so damn good at that."

He shot her a crooked grin. "Good. Maybe you'll come back for more."

Something flickered in the depths of her eyes, and she pulled him up her body. He slowly withdrew his fingers from her pussy and painted her wetness on her inner thigh, raising another shiver in her.

140

"You never shaved today." She rasped her fingers over his jawline.

"Got lazy."

"That's the second time you've called yourself lazy to me. You're far from lazy, Wheeler. Now kiss me."

She didn't need to ask him twice.

* * * * *

Damn, this man could kiss. And he knew just how to make that spot inside her bloom with want. Her insides hummed, and she ached to get him inside her. To feel his weight moving over her, that big chest pinning her and making her feel so safe and sheltered from the world.

For two days, he'd given that to her—a stranger who crashed into his peaceful life, and still he'd let her in, offered her everything he had including his trust.

Men like that just didn't exist anymore.

In a time of alarm systems and guard dogs, Wheeler had left her alone in his house and gone off to King's. He'd fed her even when his rations were spare, and he hadn't batted an eye when she asked him to keep her secret under wraps, when so many would run straight to a telephone and call a news station to say they knew of her whereabouts.

Wheeler was completely different.

And yet so familiar.

141

Maybe it was the mark of a cowboy on him that gave her a sense of homecoming. Or the fact he was cut from the same bolt of cloth the men in her life were — her daddy and her momma's brothers, the trainers, wranglers and so many others who had supported the ranch she'd grown up on.

Wheeler pulled away from the kiss, panting as he stared down into her eyes. "I want to make this last, honey, but if I don't get inside you soon, I'm going to lose my mind."

Her eyes fluttered shut on the compliment, and she wrapped her arms tighter around him. With a low groan, he buried his face against her neck. The intimacy of the moment and the idea of her returning to her life in a few hours was enough to make her decision.

"I'll come back and I'll bring condoms." She ruffled the hair on the back of his head.

He made a noise in his throat and curled closer. "You won't have to — I'll have a semi-truck back up to the door and deliver them as soon as I can make the call."

A giggle left her, and the strangely emotional moment fled, to be replaced by him delivering a playful pinch to her nipple.

They rolled. She got his clothes off and wet her lips when she set eyes on his impressive length. Tracing a vein down the side to the base, she watched his eyes darken with need.

"Tell me you got the condom out of the truck," she said.

"In my jeans." His Adam's apple worked in his throat.

She reached out and snagged his jeans. Locating the condom was easy — it was her shaking fingers that made opening the packet difficult.

"Gimme it." He stuck it in his teeth and ripped.

Fresh arousal flooded her at the sexy-as-hell action of the hottest man she'd ever met.

He jerked the condom on in one flick of his wrist and dragged her down on the blanket again. Cupping her face tenderly in one broad palm, he kissed her. Softly at first and letting it build, taking her from desire to bone-shattering need in a heartbeat. By the time he settled her over his hips, with her pussy poised at the tip of his thick cock, her emotions were back in place, all tangled up with the fun of the moment.

With his gaze locking her in place, he took hold of her hips and shoved her downward at the moment he pushed up. His cock stretched her, and she cried out at the sensations running through her system.

Every jerk of his hips drove her too high too fast. She didn't want the moment to end. Wanted to keep hiding here with him and finding herself again.

A shock tore through her.

That was it. She'd lost a little of herself between working with horses on the set of *Redemption Falls* and getting in front of the camera. Where she belonged was with the land, the animals.

And this man was most definitely fitting the bill for her. Jason Lee who?

She took Wheeler's mouth and fed him her tongue. He growled out his response and locked her against him, fucking her slow and deep.

When she felt his muscles stiffen, she knew he was close and damn if her body didn't react. Her orgasm hit out of nowhere, a pounding bliss that overtook her brain and yanked a scream from her lips.

As he hollered his own release, she opened her eyes to look down at his handsome face twisted in ecstasy. And he was looking back at her.

* * * * *

Wheeler was sick of these crutches, that was for damn sure. His frustration level was at an all-time high, and he knew why.

Aria was gone.

For two days he'd been on his own, and he'd been attempting to manage the chores alone. The irritation of trying to lead horses while leaning on one crutch was bad enough without the echoes of Aria following him around ever freakin' corner he turned.

The ranch felt empty without her.

144

He found it damn odd, too. It was like having a stray cat show up and feeding it for two days and then when it left again, he missed it.

It felt just as fleeting, passing through, enriching his life for a blink of time and then vanishing once more.

He hadn't heard from her but dropping her at the set had been a wrench to his heart. The word smitten didn't begin to cover how he was feeling about the woman. What had begun as a small ache in the center of his chest had spread until he felt pretty fucking miserable, with the bad temper to match.

He'd started using only one crutch, but he swapped it for the shovel instead. Cleaning the stalls would keep his mind off things and kill some time before he needed to head into town to the doctor. Hard to believe it hadn't' been a full week since he'd broken his foot. He hoped to hell the doc saw how desperate he was to get onto a walking cast and took mercy on him.

Of course, Wheeler was kidding himself, but a man could dream, right?

If I was gonna dream, it would be about a curvy brunette pinned against a wall.

He was fine on his own, had been his whole life. So why now was he feeling so down and despondent about being alone? Maybe if he had work to do, he wouldn't mind so much. But maybe his work had covered the loneliness for a long time and he was just now realizing it.

Either way, he needed to see how King felt about him working again, using the ATV. He'd head up there as soon as possible.

At least the horse was improving. He'd heard of pain and swelling rebounding like that, but since their night of icing the leg, it had continued to improve steadily the past two days. Now Gusto seemed to be tolerating the sprain better.

When the stall was mucked out, he filled the hay rack, made certain the horses had enough water and feed and made his slow way back to the house.

Entering the space gave him a pang, because it was far too easy to see Aria in all the rooms. Her ghost trailed him from kitchen to bedroom to living room, where he heard her tell him to prop up his foot.

Everything he did, the food he ate—hell, the air he breathed—was now connected to Aria.

He'd considered going into town and finding some gas station magazines to give him the scoop on her, but he couldn't bring himself to read third-party information. He wanted to hear from her own sweet lips how she was faring and if she'd set things to rights after running away.

It was brave of her, he'd give her that. To stand up and announce you made a mistake and then make apologies took courage. He wished he'd been there to witness it.

A couple times he'd picked up the phone to call King and see if he had any info from Bellarose, but he'd put down the phone again. He wasn't going to ask about her. It was enough that King and Bellarose thought something more was happening between him and Aria.

'Course, there was. What had their time together been to her? Only a distraction, a way to forget her problems? He'd considered that she'd slept with him to completely break ties with her ex, a way to exorcise him from her memory.

At times, Wheeler wondered… when she looked at him while in the throes of passion… Well, if it could be more.

Because he was slowly coming to realize it had been more to him. Plenty more.

He was half in love with the woman. And if she came walking through that door right this moment, the rest of his heart would follow.

A man who could give her more, what she deserved, would drive down to the set of the show, grab her and show her what she meant to him. But he didn't have the backing.

Part of his mind spoke up, whispering that King didn't have everything perfect when Bellarose came into his life. Hell, she'd been the one to buy his first horse for training. The others had soon followed, and they'd achieved King's dream together, meanwhile learning it was Bellarose's dream as well.

Aria was a rancher's daughter, appreciated hard work and good stock. But he'd seen the appreciation on her face when she looked around King's spread compared to Wheeler's. There was no comparison, unless you favored eighties décor in the house and a barn that could house more horses.

She'd told him she let choices be made for her, that life had taken over and she'd allowed it to happen. Was he guilty of the same?

When was the last time he'd dreamed of something, set a goal for himself? He was moving through life with an attitude of 'good enough,' and maybe good enough just wasn't enough anymore.

Before Aria, an old dirt road and a sunset had been a pleasure for him. Now, he didn't want those things without her.

Shit, he wasn't only half in love. He was all in— boots, hat and everything between.

In a week, his entire world had shifted on its axis. He'd lost some, gained a lot.

If he could have Aria, that was.

Tucking his crutch beneath his arm, he went back out to the shed and grabbed a sledgehammer. It was time he made some choices of his own, starting with that ugly blue countertop in his kitchen, though oh, there were sweet memories of him kissing her against it.

* * * * *

"Aria."

148

She turned at her name. It took a second for her mind to clear out the memories of Wheeler, touching her, tipping her head back to kiss her, before she realized her assistant stood before her holding a pile of fluffy towels.

"Ready for your massage?"

"Uh, yeah. Give me a minute please." She gave her the barest smile. Since her return, everyone had been beyond kind to her, so much so that she felt guiltier. She didn't deserve to be treated to massages and gifts of chocolates or good local wines. But everyone from actors to grips who hauled things around the set were treating her with care.

She'd kicked off her apologies by making that phone call to Jason. He hadn't accepted her call — the first time. But when he finally called her back, she had given the heartfelt apology he deserved. Things weren't exactly right between them, but she hoped in time he would recover and go on with his life. He was a good man and deserved more, and she'd told him so.

Then she'd gathered every single person who worked on the set of *Redemption Falls* and made a speech to them, apologizing for worrying them, scaring them. And explaining how wrong she'd been to handle the situation the way she had.

This had taken a burden off her chest, and she'd ended up in her trailer in tears. Bellarose had been sweet and come to her, caring for her like a big sister would and talking it out with plenty of hugs and finally a slice of rich cheesecake. Which made everything better.

Aria still felt overly sensitive, though, like she'd just been in a car wreck, and she'd flipped end over end until she didn't know which way was up.

All she knew was Wheeler had centered her once before, and she needed to get to him again.

The sun had risen three times since she'd seen him, and the start of each day had given her a pang. Instead of getting easier to deal with, it was more difficult. What had he been doing? Certainly not following doctor's orders, she knew that much. How was his foot and how was Gusto? Had the swelling been kept at bay? Bellarose had told her he'd started back on Blackwater, using the ATV to get around.

Calling him had seemed a pale alternative for showing up herself, but she'd been playing catchup since returning to the set. There were scripts to learn, scenes that had not been shot because of her absence and needed to be executed quickly to remain on schedule.

She'd been trying not to think too much on the situation with Wheeler. Each time he popped into her mind, it was accompanied by a leap of excitement in her chest, and frankly, it was scaring her how much she longed to see him.

Rebound, she'd heard that word enough in celebrity circles. One star changes out for another as often as they change their designer undies. That wasn't her, and she couldn't drag Wheeler into something that would hurt him.

She respected him far too much to do that.

Cared for him.

When she went to the small space in the trailer where towels had been laid over the padded massage table, she hesitated in the doorway. This was an hour of her time she could spend another way.

Looking to her assistant, she said, "I think I'm going to cancel on this, if you don't mind."

"Oh. Of course. Whatever you want, Aria."

"It's just that there's something I've been wanting to do, and I have just enough time. Do you think you can get me a car instead?"

Her assistant gave a wide smile and nodded. Ten minutes later, Aria was behind the wheel, following the GPS on her phone down into town. The small, quaint place reminded her of her home in Montana, stirring her with nostalgia. A library with a sign for kids' reading hour, a church with a bright white steeple, grocery store, gas station.

Drugstore.

She pulled in and parked the car. Then she reached over and grabbed her ballcap off the passenger's seat. With it tugged down low over her eyes, she hoped to be less recognizable than she was in the cowgirl hat she preferred. Since everybody knew her from *Redemption Falls,* she needed to look as far from that character as she could.

A glance in the mirror encouraged her that she could enter the drugstore, get what she wanted and leave without being recognized.

Inside was like any drugstore in America, and she browsed the aisles, picking up things she didn't need so it didn't appear that she was here with one thing in mind. Though it was the only thing on her mind since the moment Wheeler had grabbed her and kissed her days ago.

She located the condoms and dropped the biggest box she could find into her basket. Then she beelined it for the checkout. The clerk passed over the items without even looking at Aria, and relief hit full force when she managed to pay with cash and get out of the store without signing any autographs.

She was just setting the bag on the seat when she looked up and saw it. Wheeler's truck, across the street and empty.

Her heart gave a wild jerk in her chest, and she had to lean on the car for a moment, forcing herself to breathe steadily.

In, out, Aria. Just like you've always done.

Except Wheeler was nearby, and she had approximately forty minutes left—and a big box of condoms.

How many of them could they use before she had to return to the set?

She took off across the street, barely needing to look both directions since it was such a quiet town.

When she reached Wheeler's truck, she laid a hand on the hood. Still warm, which meant he'd just gotten here and would likely take a while in the doctor's office. Indecision struck—stay or go? Pop inside the office and see if she could find him? Or leave him a cute note on his dashboard as a surprise when he wrapped up?

She wanted to see him—bad. She'd wait. Leaning on the side, she watched the few people on the street as they visited various shops. Across the way was a tack shop. She hadn't been inside one of those in far too long. A quick browse would kill some time and by the time she was finished, Wheeler would be out. She'd be fast so she didn't miss him.

The shop was tiny and pristinely neat, each item having its own place. She admired hand-tooled tack that made her long to send a gift to her parents. She skimmed a fingertip over the artistic leatherwork but continued browsing, her mind on Wheeler. When she came across a gorgeous saddle, she paused to gape at it a moment. It was from a small shop in Texas, probably the best saddle she'd ever seen as far as craftsmanship went.

Another few minutes and she was eager to wait for Wheeler again. The shop bell trilled behind her as she hurried out, and she stepped onto the street, coming face-to-face with the gorgeous cowboy.

Her heart flipped over at the sight of his ruggedly handsome features. He'd shaved and the red shirt he wore accentuated his coloring and molded to his broad shoulders and chest.

His throat mottled with redness as he met her stare. "Aria, what are you doing here?"

"I was in town getting some things and I saw your truck. I thought I'd wait for you, but I popped into the tack shop." She waved a hand at the storefront, as if he didn't know the shop was situated here.

His jaw tightened, that tendon twitching in the crease as he stepped up to her. His stare traveled over her hair and face, down her body and back up, leaving her breathless and wanting to rip all her clothes off.

Inching closer, she squeezed her hands into fists to keep from pulling him against her and kissing those hard—yet so soft—lips.

"Christ, Aria. I want to put my hands on you so fucking bad."

His words slithered through her, landing between her thighs in a warm knot. She searched his eyes. "I was thinking the same thing."

"How have you been?" he grated out.

"I'm okay. Better, actually. It was good to apologize to everyone and take responsibility for what I did. How's the foot?"

"Two more weeks before doc clears me for a walking cast. I can't wait to chuck these into the fire and watch them burn." He wiggled the crutches.

She gave a low laugh. "I'd like to watch that." She gave him her sternest look. "You better follow his instructions."

"Thought about taking the snippers to the cast too."

"Don't you dare!"

He grunted but didn't offer any agreement on the matter. Then she saw a scrape along his wrist, just freshly scabbed.

"What did you do?" She reached to touch his arm, and he jerked at her touch. God, they were both as jumpy as kids who'd just experienced their first kiss. Not knowing if they should touch, wanting to so badly.

"Just work around the house. It's nothing."

"Doesn't sound like you're staying off your foot, and I know you've been working up at King's." Her words fell away.

His eyes darkened, and a long heartbeat stretched between them. He opened his mouth to speak, but a man down the street called out his name. Wheeler didn't look up till the second call.

"Dammit," he said faintly. Aria looked up at him but turned to face the man. An older gentleman in a canvas jacket and tan cowboy hat, dusty boots and all the hard, weathered skin of a man who spent a lifetime in the elements working with cattle. He also was bent at the shoulders under some invisible weight.

Wheeler stuck out his hand as the man reached them. They shook, but the man had his attention on Aria. "What a pleasure to see such a lovely young woman on my trip to town."

"Spence Wood, this is a friend of mine, Aria. Aria, Spence's been a friend of my family since I was in diapers."

"Well, son, that statement makes me feel damn old. Pardon my language, miss." He turned and shook her hand as well. When he retained her fingers a second too long, he gave her a smile. "A woman who knows horses. I can tell by the calluses."

She grinned, and he returned the gesture, though she noted how his happiness didn't quite stretch to his eyes. Something was troubling the man.

"Maybe you heard of my problems, Wheeler."

"Not that I can think," he responded.

"Well, I heard of yours, young man. You're lucky you didn't break your neck and not just your foot. How's the horse?"

"Sprain's gonna take a while to heal, but we're hopeful for a good outcome." Wheeler shot Aria a glance.

The man went on, "I'm finally giving it up this year."

A beat of silence followed. "Givin' it up?" Wheeler echoed.

"Yeah, I've been in a sinking ship with ranchin' for four or five years now. I just can't hold on any longer, and my wife's had some issues with her health. We're pullin' out, moving to Spokane to be closer to good doctors, and I'm sellin' it all."

Wheeler let out a low whistle and shook his head. "Damn, that's hard. I'm sorry to hear it."

"Ranchin' ain't the business it used to be, and I'm getting along in years. Not training the reining horses as much. You wouldn't be in the market for a good pair, would ya?" He eyed Wheeler.

At the mention of reining horses, Aria sucked in a gasp and held it.

"They aren't that old, just getting them started really, but they're showing real promise."

"Man, I'd love to jump on that opportunity."

"Could use the cash, if I'm honest," Spence went on.

Wheeler pressed his lips together and shook his head. "Being laid up this way, I'm in my own tough predicament and I can't spare the money. Even so, I'm not sure I could afford that pair, knowing what they must be worth."

"I'd like to help you out, but—"

Aria took a step forward. "We'll take them. Give me a price and I'll have a check for you in an hour."

The man's mouth dropped open, and he stared at her. "Why, here's a filly who knows her mind. Wheeler, where you been hiding this gem? I feel like I know you from somewhere, young lady."

"I get that a lot," she said with a smile. "I'm serious that we'll take the horses." She felt Wheeler's heavy stare on her and threw him a nervous smile.

He named a price and she arched a brow. "Seems like you're low-balling me."

Spence chuckled. "This is a sharp one, for sure. It's a fair offer for liquidation. Take it or leave it, young lady."

"I'll take it," she said at once.

"Well, that's real good news. I'm glad to see them go to a good home with people who know what they're worth. Let me give you a card with my number." He fished into his wallet and came out with a white business card with his ranch logo on it as well as his phone number and address. "You can pick them up there at the address too. Just call ahead first, if ya would. Sometimes my wife's got appointments."

"Of course." She stuck out her hand, and he shook on the deal. "Thank you."

* * * * *

The second Spence was out of earshot, Wheeler grabbed Aria's arm and pulled her over. Bending to her ear, he said, "Did you just buy two very expensive horses?"

"Uh-huh. I'm excited!"

"Aria."

She turned those big brown eyes on him.

He couldn't hold back.

"Fuck." He slammed his mouth over hers, breaking away as quickly as he'd kissed her but wanting so much more.

"Wheeler!"

"I'm sorry. I shouldn't kiss you in public — there's probably someone taking pictures right now. I shouldn't have done it, but…" He locked his stare on her ripe lips and damn if he wasn't gonna kiss her again if he didn't do something fast.

He hobbled a few feet to his truck, whipped open the door and ushered her in. She slid onto the seat and he slammed the door before moving to the driver's side. Here, they were still in plain sight, so he couldn't lunge for her and thrust his tongue down her throat, but at least they weren't standing on the sidewalk for anybody with a phone to snap their photo.

She twisted in the seat, a grin lighting her beautiful features. "What a lucky buy that was! Who would ever give up a pair of reining horses that have already begun their training for that price?"

"Oh God." She really didn't see a problem, did she?

"What's wrong?"

"Aria. You can't buy those horses and put them on my land."

Her face fell. Finally, he was getting through to her. He didn't view her as impetuous, but now he

159

was beginning to wonder if the running away from her wedding thing, the buying pricey horses on the spot thing, was just Aria.

"Oh. I wasn't thinking about you needing some updates to your barn. Those stall doors could be replaced and of course, the new horses will need a new run."

"Yeah. And I work full time on Blackwater—or I will be in a coupla months. I don't have time to drop everything and train horses."

"I'll do it." She said this so simply that he believed her—almost.

He took her hand—no use in holding back any longer. "Honey, you have a full-time job too. When are you coming up to train those horses? And how am I building the run or stall doors when I'm on crutches?" It was one thing to tear out the countertop, as he'd been doing all week, but demolition was a sight easier than rebuilding.

She turned her hand up in his and threaded their fingers. The warm hit to his heart nearly had his eyes shutting. "Wheeler, that rancher needed help. We took the horses off his hands, and now he has money to help his wife."

"So you did this purely as an act of altruism?"

She shrugged. "I can't stand a sad story without stepping in to help. And I admit it was somewhat selfish of me, since reining horses is what I always wanted to compete with. I know that time is past me now, but the training I still love, and I can see it done. The horses could be good earners for you."

He didn't know whether to laugh at her crazy idea or pinch the bridge of his nose in consternation. She was impulsive and insane but so earnest and excited that he couldn't help but bring her hand to his lips. When he skimmed his mouth over her knuckles, she sucked in a breath.

"I have no damn clue what to do, woman, but now you've purchased two horses, and we need a place to house them. I might be able to see if King has some leftover lumber I could—"

She pressed her fingertip to his lips. "Leave it to me. Oh crap, is that the time?" She glanced at his dash.

"Yeah."

"I'm due on set in ten minutes. I'm playing catchup. But Wheeler... what if I come to you tonight? Could I?"

Hell, she was actually asking if he wanted her? How could she even wonder such a thing?

"Pretty sure I'll be home, honey."

She cupped his jaw, looking into his eyes. "Good. Don't worry about getting... um, supplies. I've already picked those up."

His eyes bulged. "Do you mean—?"

She reached for the door handle and started to slide out.

"Aria!" He lashed his fingers around her wrist, holding her a minute longer.

"I gotta run, Wheeler. I've got a lot to do. Oh! And you wouldn't mind running some lines with me tonight, would you? The writers have made some changes and I don't quite have them all memorized." She pulled away.

"Aria, wait, dammit." His tone brought her to a halt.

Across the seat, she stared at him, a crinkle between her brows. "What is it?"

"This." He stretched the distance and captured her lips in a kiss, taking control just as he felt her give herself up to him. He probed her lips and deeper, stroking his tongue over hers only a few times before she hummed her delight.

Just as she began to respond, he withdrew, thumbing her lips with the pad of his thumb. "Go. I'll be waiting for you."

She flashed a grin.

"And just so you know, I'm gonna suck at running lines."

"I know." She giggled and closed the door. He watched her jog across the street, shaking his head. What was he going to do with that woman?

Grab on with both hands and hold on tight for the ride.

162

Chapter Eight

Halfway up Wheeler's driveway, Aria's nerves hit.

She was feeling a bit wishy-washy about the horse deal. She'd made a decision, but was it the right one?

It was the leap of interest she'd seen in Wheeler's eyes when Spence offered him the pair of horses that had spurred her to jump on the chance to buy them. For once, she'd seen something Wheeler wanted, if only he had the means.

That she could help with.

And, if she was honest, she had wanted those horses. Suddenly her own abandoned hopes had rushed to the surface, and she just couldn't walk away and regret sitting on the fence.

Now, she was wondering if she'd been too rash. Sure, she'd thought of the logistics — housing, training, cost to feed. But the future was uncertain. She owned horses that would be housed on Wheeler's land. On the surface, it was a good business transaction, but they both knew more than partnership was at work between them.

Her emotions were like roots, burrowing deeper by the hour she knew the sexy cowboy. But if things went south, what then? He wouldn't want her horses on his land.

When she saw the cabin, she peered closer at it. What was stacked outside? She couldn't make out what the strange bars of blue were. She parked the truck near the barn so the lumber in the back would be easily unloaded once the guys from the lumber store got here.

She was just climbing out when she spotted Wheeler coming out of the barn. One look at him had her stomach fluttering with joy.

"You came." His low tone made her think he hadn't believed she would. He slanted a look at the truck. "What the..."

She stepped up to him and tilted her head to look into his eyes. "I have to apologize to you, Wheeler."

"What for?"

"I didn't consult with you about the horses. I just bought them, without thought to our arrangement."

He slid an arm around her back, tugging her closer. "Why don't we negotiate now?" Before she could draw in a breath, he planted his mouth over hers.

The flavor of man and desire permeated her head, and she embraced all the tingles that went along with it. Her body stirred to life as she angled her head so he could probe his tongue deeper into her mouth.

A small groan rumbled through his chest, and she wiggled closer. The brush of hard muscle against sensitive nipples had her fires blazing after three passes of his tongue. She clung to his neck, swayed into his hold, and kissed him with all the fervor she'd kept bottled up over the past few days.

Breaking away, she met his stare. "If that kiss means we split the ownership of the horses, then that's exactly what I was thinking."

"Uh-huh." He flattened his palm over her spine, hauling her flush to his body. Need spiked, and she rubbed against the bulge in his jeans.

"They're on my land, so I supply the feed."

"No. I provide feed as part of the boarding cost."

"You give too much, honey."

"Then you're not angry with me for buying the horses without your say?"

"Well, I would have preferred to do things a bit differently, but I see how happy this makes you."

A warmth spread across her insides, like honey on hot bread. She pulled back to meet his gaze, pleased that he wanted to make her happy. "But does it make *you* happy? I saw how much you wanted those horses, Wheeler."

"I did," he grated out. "But I want you more." He went for her mouth again, claiming her lips and tongue like he planned to do this the rest of his days.

Her heart gave a wild leap at the thought.

165

As he put both arms around her, his crutch hit the ground. She laughed against his lips, and he swept her up, turning on his good foot and pinning her to the side of the barn.

"Oh God, I want you," she rasped.

He ripped open her pants and spun her to face the wall. With her hands braced to support herself before her knees buckled, she gave herself up to him. He bit into her earlobe as he nudged her jeans and panties down her hips. Then he latched onto her neck and cupped her by the pussy.

"You're fucking drenched. Did you want me?"

"Told you I did," she said faintly as he sucked at a sensitive spot on her throat.

He rocked his hips, pressing his erection into her ass. "Can you tell I want you just as bad?"

He swirled his tongue up and down her throat, and she barely registered the sound of his zipper, when all of a sudden she felt the head of his hard cock probing at her slick folds from behind.

A deep throb took up residence in her pussy. She angled her ass back, pressing against him for more. For all of him.

Now.

"Take me, Wheeler."

"Fuck, I don't have a condom."

"Front pocket of my jeans. I just need to feel you stretching me. Please."

"Hell." His voice grated over her senses, and a minute after, he located everything he needed and slid home in one long glide.

The insane pleasure of having him sent her stomach into backflips. She reached around to grab his nape and draw him back to her throat. A rough grunt left him as he sagged at the knees, almost lifting her on his cock. She cried out. He pulled out and shoved deep again.

Her insides clutched at every inch of him. When he knotted her hair in his fist and angled her head the other way so he could kiss that side of her throat, need exploded. She shoved back. His cock hit the innermost spot inside her, and she wanted more.

He sucked on her neck, fucking with precise jerks of his hips that were going to drive her to the brink of insanity.

No, she was already there.

He drew her head around and landed a kiss on her mouth. The seeking tongue plunging between her lips was all she needed to send her sharply up the slope toward ecstasy.

A long moan left her, and her pussy clenched on him. Pulsing hard and fast.

He answered with a growl, and it was all it took. She came. Waves hit, and she was helpless against them. She let them swallow her, clinging to the wall while he plunged in again and again.

When she gave a final cry, he yanked out. "Fuck, I can't come yet. I want to make it last."

She gathered her wits swiftly, realizing he'd give her all the pleasure and taken none for himself. She turned into his arms. A glance down showed her that he gripped his cock at the base and a glance up revealed how hard he was battling his control. Jaw clamped shut, brows creased.

She dropped to her knees before him and cupped his balls in one hand. She worked off the condom and stroked him through her fist ten times, twelve. A desperate sound left his throat as he guided his cock to her lips.

She parted for him and swallowed the warm length.

He let his head droop, eyes hooded as he watched her pleasure him. "Fuck, honey. You sure you can take me? When I blow..."

She smiled around his thickness. He braced a hand on the wall and one on the back of her head, feeding her his hard cock with rhythmic twitches of his hips.

Closing her eyes, she let him sink into her mouth and beyond. The tip of his erection probed the back of her throat, and she swallowed reflexively.

"Hell. Here it comes. Oh fuck, honey, your mouth..." He stiffened. His cock hardened in her mouth before erupting. Spurts hit her tongue, and she swallowed again. Tasting man and his sweet essence as he gave himself up to her.

At that moment, she realized just how happy she wanted to make him too.

As the last pulse of juices hit her tongue, Wheeler curled forward. Tenderness struck, and she slowly let him go and slid to her feet, gathering him close.

He folded her against him, cupping the back of her head and bringing her lips to his once more.

The moment stretched on.

When he drew away, his eyes burned with an intensity she hadn't seen before. It reached out and captured her heart.

Suddenly, he raised his head, listening. "Is that an engine I hear?"

"The guys from the lumber store coming to unload the wood for us."

"I could have managed. You've done enough."

"You can't manage with crutches. Now let me do what I can here, Wheeler. But you'd better zip your fly and I'd like to have my jeans back in place before they show up."

"Shit." He let her go and bent to retrieve his jeans and boxers. While he fixed his belt, he eyed her in the hungry way of a predator and its prey.

"You look like you want to take me again already."

"I do. Your lips are swollen from sucking my cock, and I can't stop staring at you."

Electric heat washed through her. Somehow, she managed to right her clothing just as she heard the truck come to a stop in the driveway.

Glancing down, she made sure she was completely clothed and hadn't forgotten anything — her muddled brain would make it easy enough to forget. But both of them were presentable.

Except...

"Did you chop your jeans off at the knee?"

"Yeah, this pair wasn't fitting around my cast so easily, so I took the knife to it."

She giggled.

"What, it's not a good look?"

"One half of you looks like a cowboy and the other a castaway."

"If you wanna play pirates, later, I'm down with that." He flashed her a grin and headed around the barn with his crutch.

For a moment, Aria stood there, leaning against the wall, letting her mind catch up to everything that was happening. And wondering how, in such a short time, she'd managed to find all the things she'd ever wanted right here on a small ranch in the mountains of Washington.

* * * * *

170

"Don't go." Wheeler brushed his lips over the crest of Aria's breast. The tip puckered, and he gave it a gentle lick, raising a moan from her.

"I have to be on set."

"Bellarose stays at her place and goes down in the morning to film," he rumbled against her smooth skin.

"And they're married."

He locked her in his stare. The words on his lips — right there.

Marry me then.

He couldn't say them and put her into another bad situation, and definitely not so soon. Hell, she'd just gotten done running from a different man who'd wanted to bind her to him. Aria was the type of woman who made men lose their heads, and Wheeler was officially one of them.

"It's not that late," he cajoled. "Besides, didn't you say you want to run lines?"

"Oh yeah."

He scraped his teeth lightly over her nipple before pushing onto his knees. Aria was spread out on his bed, looking languid and sexy as hell after he'd just given her three more orgasms. He smirked with satisfaction.

"What's that for?" she asked.

"Now your lips are really puffy from all the attention I've given them. Guess that means they're mine now."

Her eyes softened, and she ran a hand over his pec. "Will you grab my script? It's folded up in my jeans pocket."

"Sure." He climbed off the bed and fumbled to grab his crutch. He made his way to the bathroom to clean up, and when he returned he got the script. She was sitting up, leaning against a pile of pillows, and the sheet was tucked under her arms, covering her nudity from him.

She couldn't look lovelier. And Wheeler was pretty far gone now. The lust he'd felt from the start had mellowed into something sweeter, more desperate, and he had a feeling that something was love.

He lay next to her and handed her the script. She unfolded the sheets of paper and read them over. He closed his eyes a second, just drinking in her nearness. He loved having her here. Even when she scolded him about doing too much work on his kitchen by removing all the countertops, he ached for more.

"Okay. I'm Fallon and you can read the parts of Braxton."

"Braxton." He snorted. "Pussy name."

"Not everyone can have a name as tough as Wheeler. Okay, I think I'm ready." She passed him the pages, and he stared at the lines.

"Fallon, will you just stop for a second? Think about what you're doing—to this ranch. To us."

She pushed out a sigh, and he saw the moment she was in character. Stunned, he couldn't look away from her. "The ranch means everything to me. But I just can't spend my life here, fighting with my relatives over what our father wanted for us. This was his dream."

"It could be yours too."

"It is—but it's a different sort of dream. I'd do everything so differently..."

"Those words were off. Are they supposed to be exact?"

"Crap. What are they again?"

He read the lines, and she repeated them twice.

On the pages, it said Braxton moved closer to her. Now *that* Wheeler could get on board with.

He shifted, covering her with his body.

"What are you doing?"

"Gettin' in character." He lowered his hips to hers, settling his erection at the notch of her legs with the thin barrier of the sheet between them.

"Mmm, I'm on board with this." She grabbed his buttocks, and he rocked into her again.

She ground back, and he felt the liquid heat of her even through the cotton.

Staring into his eyes, she said, "What are my next lines?"

"I think they were something about me taking you."

Her lips, a breath away, curved up. "Is that so?"

"Yeah. I think it says something about you begging me to tongue your pussy." Leaning away, he pinched the sheet and dragged it to the side.

"God, I hope it says that."

He flashed her a grin and slithered down her body. Parting her thighs, he wet his lips. "What's your next line?"

"I think it was along the lines of 'Please lick my pussy, you hot, hunky cowboy.'"

Using his thumbs, he spread her plump labia to expose her straining clit and drenched inner folds. "I hope it says I don't come up for air until you scream my name."

She gripped his hair and pressed him downward. "Running lines with you is..." her breath hitched as he sank his tongue deep "...definitely more fun than with anyone else."

"Nobody else gets to touch you, honey. You're all mine." Closing his eyes, he opened his mouth and claimed her.

* * * * *

Wheeler gave Gusto's neck a soft stroke. "You're healin' slowly but surely, aren't you, boy? Doin' good. Real good."

The past three weeks had shown a lot of changes around the place, but best of all was how Gusto seemed steadier on that injured leg. The vet had come

174

and gone for his weekly checks, and he praised Wheeler for all he'd achieved in his care. Wheeler sure couldn't take credit for all of it, not when Aria had done so much in the beginning.

Now that she was back on set for long hours, he tended the horse himself, and he'd figured out ways to maneuver on his single crutch to make things easier, such as adding an extension to the garden hose to run cold water to the bucket instead of carrying the bucket to the horse. Soaking the leg had become a routine Gusto didn't mind anymore either, and it helped that the horse was so cooperative.

The builders Aria had hired were also nearly completed with the long run and a few gates the horses would need for training. And Wheeler had managed to hang new stall doors in time for Spence to deliver the horses.

He lifted his head and looked out across the fence at them. Standing side by side, the mares were proud and born for competition. Last time she'd been here, Aria had spouted off a list of things she needed to do with the stock on her day off and he'd only shaken his head at her, right before cornering her and telling her that she wasn't going to be training these horses on her days off, because she would be in bed with him all day.

To that, she'd laughed. But when he'd stolen the first kiss, she'd caved and by the time she was panting out her first release, she'd agreed they would hire someone.

"Wheeler?"

He stumped over to the fence to see King coming his way, shock written on his face. "Holy shit. When did you do this?"

"It's been a work in progress."

King came to a dead stop as he spotted the new stock. "Hell. Are those reining horses?"

"Yeah."

"Spence's stock."

"They were Spence's stock."

King's brows flew upward. "You bought them?"

"Aria did."

King's eyes bulged. "Aria. What the hell is happening around here?"

Wheeler leaned on the fence, and King drifted up to the other side, taking in all the improvements.

"Why didn't you say? You've been at Blackwater every day and didn't say a word." King gave a shake of his head.

He shrugged. "It felt kinda personal. I don't know how to describe it."

"Personal how?" He eyed Wheeler, far too good of a friend to ignore the things Wheeler wasn't saying.

"It's hard to describe."

"Personal because you're in love with her."

That pretty much summed it up. He nodded and picked at a splinter on the fence rail.

"This is big, man. You're setting up to train horses together."

"It's a dream of Aria's. She's always trained horses, and she couldn't pass up these when Spence offered them. I'm just part of the deal, boarding them for her."

"Uh-huh. I'm sure that's it."

Wheeler nudged his hat up. "I don't know how she feels."

"But you want more."

"I'd like that, yeah. But…"

A long second passed, and King leaned his elbows on the rail. "But what?"

"I can't give her what she deserves. Hell, I feel bad enough about her buying the lumber and hiring guys to build onto the fence and create the run. I barely scraped enough to install new butcher block counters in my kitchen, and it will take months for me to save enough to update the bathroom."

"Damn, bro. You've got it bad. Finally working on this place to make it cozy for a woman?"

"You're not helping, King."

He huffed out a laugh. "I'm sure I'm not. It's just that I've been through this before. Wanting to give your woman the universe but on a rancher's budget."

"I'm not even a rancher. Just a cowpoke who's been stingy enough over the years to save a little."

"You're right—I don't know what Aria would see in you. Bum foot, in need of a haircut. Pretty ugly to look at." King grinned.

"You're a dick."

"I know. So when are you gonna pop the question?"

He shook his head. "Can't. She's just run from a wedding, remember?"

"Yeah, one that was being forced on her by a man she didn't want."

"Who knows if I'm what she wants? No, I can't take things further. We're just enjoying each other for now. It hasn't even been very long."

"You realize the filming will wrap up in another month's time and Aria will go back to Hollywood."

King's words were a sharp jab to his heart. Wheeler gnawed at his lower lip before giving a nod. "I guess I'll just have to hope…"

"Hope that you grow a pair of balls before then? Dude, coming from the voice of experience, if you don't act soon… if you let her go… you'll regret it more than anything you've ever regretted in your life. You gotta tell her how you feel."

Wheeler stood there a moment, stricken with dread at the very thought of Aria walking away from him forever. Of course, he'd never believed it could be more than just sex and a mutual love for horses. Now…

He glanced up at King. "You're right. I have to tell her."

"Don't wait too long." He waved at the new pair of horses. "Money to be made here. I just heard about a million dollar rider in the junior reining division."

"That's Aria's goal."

"Achievable." He looked at Wheeler hard. "And so is yours. Grab that woman and don't let her go."

Wheeler couldn't stop the crooked smile from overtaking his face. "This entire situation is insane. All I did was take a fall and mess up my horse and myself. Now suddenly, I've got a pair of champion horses, updates to the barn and fence and a gorgeous woman in my bed."

King laughed and smacked Wheeler on the shoulder. "I know the feelin'. With Bellarose, she fell in love with the lifestyle of a rancher. Sounds to me like it's Aria's first love."

"It is." He hoped the second would be him.

"Then it's not hard to reason that she'd choose you, Wheeler. Need me to look at Gusto's leg while I'm here?"

The change in topic didn't faze Wheeler. He shook his head. "Nah, he's good. I just checked him and I'll ice the leg later on."

"Good deal. If you need any more help, you know where to find me."

They gripped hands in a bro-shake and then King got back in his truck, leaving Wheeler alone with his thoughts. The quiet rustle of horses as they grazed soothed his racing mind. It was too soon to share his feelings with Aria. Yet, King was right. If he let her walk away, he'd regret it forever.

What he needed was the equivalent of a promise ring to an eighth grader, something to prove his feelings were deeper than just rolling in the hay.

But what to get a woman who could buy anything she wanted?

She wasn't one for jewelry, just an occasional pair of silver studs in her earlobes. He'd never seen her carry expensive handbags, either. What did women like?

His brain stumbled over a moment in time, when he'd seen her come out of the tack shop. A woman like Aria would be into something she could use on the horses, and he'd know it when he saw it.

Guess he was making a trip back into town sooner than expected. He could stop off for some more steaks too and treat her to a nice dinner. He rubbed at his jaw. Both these things would get him laid—but would it have the effect he hoped for? He wanted nothing less than for her to rush into his arms when he confessed he was in love with her.

One worry popped up in the back of his brain, though—she'd run away once. What would stop her from running again?

Chapter Nine

When Aria slipped inside the open front door of Wheeler's house, she knew he'd be sound asleep. It was nearing midnight, and she felt terrible about showing up so late, when she'd been expected hours ago. She'd considered breaking their plans to see each other due to the late hour, and she'd fought with herself—and lost. So here she was, taking a chance that she wouldn't startle him awake and have to face down a shotgun.

He *had* left the door unlocked for her. Hopefully that meant he was waiting for her still.

She moved silently through the living room, making out the dark, bulky shapes of the sofa, chair and footstool. The scent of freshly cut wood was a sharp tang in her nostrils, and she realized he'd been at the butcherblock countertop again, probably putting on the finishing touches.

That had been a surprise when he'd begun the renovation on the counters. She'd taken him for being a passive man and just getting on with what he had because it was still serviceable. But now she realized he just might not have had the time to put into the house and make it his own.

Also, he was an outdoorsy man and now that he was trapped inside longer with his broken foot, he could have gotten tired of looking at all the things he wanted to improve around the place.

She moved past the kitchen and into the hallway, drawn to him in a way that was brand new to her.

She wanted him — to shed her clothes and glide into bed beside him, to wrap her arms around him and cuddle up close. All those things shouted out that she was in so much deeper than she'd thought.

And everything about spending time with Wheeler was the complete opposite from being with Jason.

Reaching the doorway, she paused, looking in at the cowboy fast asleep in bed. He lay on one side, face turned from her but she could make out the dark shadow of hair on his jaw. The sheet only partially covered his bare torso, and the thick cast protruded from beneath the edge of the sheet.

Her heart gave a small tug, and then she drifted forward, shedding her boots and clothes. When she was only clad in tiny panties, she lifted the sheet and slid into the cocoon of warmth given off by his body.

Muttering in his sleep, he turned over. Tenderness washed across her senses, and she wrapped an arm around him. He came awake all at once, eyes wide and staring as if he was seeing her in his dream.

Maybe he was. Her heart gave another tiny jolt.

"God." His voice was gritty with sleep. He pulled her flush against him and looked into her eyes once more before tucking her head beneath his chin. "You're here."

Snuggled close to his chest, she felt the stresses of the long day fade away and her muscles begin to relax.

"You've gotta be bushed." His chest rumbled under her ear.

"I am. But I couldn't stay away."

His throat clicked as he swallowed. "Those are the sweetest words I've heard in my time."

She smiled against his chest, brushing her fingertips over the soft hairs that sprang up. "Wheeler."

"Yeah, honey."

She tipped her head back to look at him. "Will you make love to me?"

A growl hit his lips and he curled a hand around her bare breast. "I thought you'd never ask."

She giggled. "I've only been here three minutes."

"Yeah, it was two minutes and fifty-five seconds too long for me. C'mere."

It was a lot longer before they surfaced again.

* * * * *

Wheeler eyed Aria. Standing at his new countertop wearing nothing but his T-shirt, her curvy

183

legs bare, she had his cock standing at full attention, and hell, it wasn't even rooster's crow yet.

He still couldn't believe she'd come to him in the night. He'd gone to bed with hope in his heart and the door unlocked just in case, but he hadn't believed she'd show up. Then she'd blown his mind by asking if he'd make love to her... and well, his body was going to feed off those moments for a lonnnng time.

She had to leave in a few, but she'd insisted on making him coffee before she did. Forget the coffee — the sweetest woman he could ever imagine was standing in his kitchen completely bare under his T-shirt.

Now would be a good time to talk to her. A *great* time.

Words revolved through his head. He sampled them or discarded them outright. There seemed to be no good way to go about telling a woman he loved her without risk of scaring her off.

She'd be running for the hills in seconds if he told her outright. And Wheeler hardly knew any other way to be other than straightforward.

When she turned with a fresh mug of coffee for him, she offered a tempting smile. "I can feel your eyes on me, Wheeler."

"Can't hardly keep them off you. You're so damn beautiful."

Moving close, she curled a hand around his neck and pulled him down to kiss his cheek. "I'm going to get dressed and go. I can't be late today."

"Big day for Fallon?" Her character's situations amused him.

"Yeah, she finally admits to her stepbrother she's in love with him."

Shit—he couldn't possibly tell her that now. What would he say—speaking of being in love with someone, I'm in love with you?

"Thanks for the coffee." He held her to his chest for a moment, and then she broke away and disappeared down the hall to the bedroom, hips swaying loosely from all the pleasure he'd given her the night before.

Aching to go after her, grab her and blurt out all the things in his mind, he gripped his mug tighter. He started to raise it to his mouth but quickly set it down, plucked his crutch from where it leaned on the table and rushed after her.

She turned to him with a smile and fluffed her hair free of her shirt collar. Then she saw something on his face that made her brow crease. "Wheeler?"

"I've got a surprise for you."

Her smile widened. "You do?"

"Yeah, down at the barn. Do you have time to come see?"

"Of course, but now you're tempting me with spending time with the horses, and I miss them so much."

"I promise I won't let you be late."

He already had on the jeans she'd poked fun at last time he'd worn them, and all he had to do was throw on a shirt and boot and he was ready. She followed him down to the barn. Hell, it felt so right to have her next to him. All he had to do was say three little words. Why were they lodged in his throat?

When they reached the barn, he held the door for her. She moved inside, and the horses greeted her with soft whickers.

"I promise I'll try my best to break free and come see you all," she crooned.

He hit the light and took her by the arm, turning her to look at the hay bale where the brand new saddle sat.

Her sharp intake of air stroked over his senses. She latched onto his arm. "Wheeler…"

"Guy in the tack shop said you were eyeing it when you were in."

"I… Oh my God. I can't believe you did this." She moved forward to touch the leather, running her fingers over the tooling and intricate designs cut into it.

He inched up beside her, heart thumping hard. "I wanted to give you something."

"It's amazing. Thank you!" She turned and hugged him hard before pivoting back to inspect the saddle.

I love you, that's why.

"I thought it might be a good way to seal our partnership."

She spun to face him. A heartbeat passed. "Partnership?"

"Yeah, your horses, my land. We make a good team."

"Oh."

"I mean, we'll have a good run at championships in a year or two with these horses." Why wasn't anything coming out right? *Just say it.*

He opened his mouth, but she was just staring at him.

"Yes, we will. Well… thank you, Wheeler. I love the saddle and I can't wait to use it."

A heavy weight tugged at his heartstrings. He hadn't said anything at all. What a damn coward.

"I gotta get to the set. I'll see you later?" She didn't quite meet his gaze.

He couldn't let her go like this. Reaching out, he took her arm again. "Aria…"

"Thanks for the saddle, Wheeler. I really do love it." Pulling free, she walked out of the barn.

Dammit.

* * * * *

Not even being on Blackwater, doing what work he could for King was setting Wheeler at ease today. By now the herd was getting accustomed to the ATV invading their territory, and they were surrounding him the minute he entered the field.

He moved slowly through the herd, swaying his head left and right to check the steers for signs of lameness and to see if any were lying down. The mindless task afforded him too much time to think about what he'd done wrong with Aria.

It was obvious she'd been upset when she left. When he thought on it, he knew it was the mention of a partnership that had set her off. The stiff set of her shoulders and way she'd avoided looking at him were sure signs.

By mentioning the partnership, he'd played it safe, toed the line. He'd been too much of a wimp to just spit out how he truly felt for her. Jesus, King had warned him away from doing that very thing and he'd still gone and done it. Maybe he was one of those guys who had to touch the fire to learn it was hot.

Or in this case, ice cold. He expected when he did see her again, it would take some wooing to warm her up to him again.

Determination settled into his bones. He'd do what it took and go the extra mile—hell, ten million miles—to ensure she knew exactly how he felt about her.

When he rounded the outer edge of the field, he spotted a hump on the earth. Adrenaline hit his system, and he depressed the gas, zooming toward it faster.

The steer lay on its side, gasping for air.

"Dammit."

If it had been down a while, it had bloat, and that meant the trapped gas was pressing on its lungs, making it hard for it to breathe. The real question was, could it even get up to be treated?

He braked the ATV and reached for the rope on his hip. The coil was an extension of his hand, and when he threw, the loop landed square over the steer's head. He walked up, using caution in case it had a sudden burst of energy, but the animal remained on its side. He looped the rope more securely so he could use it to pull the steer to its feet.

After a quick examination, he knew it hadn't broken a leg. It was down for some other reason, but he wasn't about to let it die on his watch.

He smacked its rump. "Get on! C'mon!"

The animal rocked in attempt to get to its feet but didn't make it. He maneuvered behind the thousand-pound steer and pushed on its back. "Yaw! Get on!"

This time it rocked more toward its stomach, a good thing since it was the only way to get its legs beneath it. He dug in his boot and pushed with all his might. The extra boost helped the steer into a better position, but it still gasped for air.

He had a bloat tube in the bag on the ATV, but first he had to get the animal up. Moving to the head, he got the rope and pulled. The steer didn't budge. After a few more attempts, he was able to get the animal to push up a bit on its forelegs.

"Get on!"

The steer tried again, and he simultaneously gave the pull of his life. Suddenly it popped up, swaying. He had to regain his own balance after the sudden shift in strength, and he planted his cast to remain upright. No pain shot through his foot, so that was a good thing.

He rushed to the bag and got the bloat tube. One jab in its hide—the steer wouldn't feel it anyway since the hide didn't have nerves—and the trapped air could get out. Wheeler approached the beast slowly again, cooing to it.

Less than a minute later, the air was draining out of the animal, ripe and fowl. Wheeler stepped back, assessing how to get it back to the barn to be looked after before releasing it to the herd once more. On horseback, it'd be nothing to lead it by the rope, but he'd never used an ATV for the task before. The steer could be just spooky enough to resist and not follow.

Nothin' to do but give it a shot. He'd gotten this far.

Taking hold of the lead rope, he hopped on the ATV again. The animal tolerated the engine noise, but when he tried to get it moving, it refused to follow behind. Thinking it could do with the smell of the exhaust, he moved the ATV to the side, keeping the rope taut horizontally. When he rolled forward, the steer began to walk alongside him, about ten feet off.

It made for some slow progress, but eventually he got the animal to the barn. He gave it a more thorough examination but couldn't find much wrong. By this time, Schmitty and King turned up.

"A call to the vet is in order. Could be summer pneumonia. The abrupt change of season causes it sometimes," Wheeler told King.

He gave a nod. "I'll call now. How'd you manage with the ATV instead of a horse?"

He laughed. "I prefer four legs to four wheels, but we managed fine."

"When's your next doctor appointment?" King eyed up Wheeler's cast. He'd stuck a knit hat over his exposed toes, but everything looked the worse for wear after walking through the pasture on it.

"Not soon enough," he responded.

"Heard you were at the tack shop yesterday." Schmitty knew all the comings and goings in town and on the outer limits.

He gave a nod. "That's right."

Schmitty shot King a shit-eating grin. "Giving a woman a saddle is equivalent to getting on bended knee. So? Did you pop the question?"

Irritated and angry with himself, Wheeler grunted. "No. I flubbed it."

King and Scmitty exchanged a look and then burst out laughing.

"Sure, poke fun at the guy who sucks with words."

"Dude, do you think we're any better? We're men. We don't talk—we take action. Your first mistake was opening your mouth," King said.

"Your second was not just grabbing her and kissing her."

Wheeler doffed his hat and raked his fingers through his hair. "I know that now. A day late and a dollar short."

"Never too late, my friend." King smacked him on the shoulder. "But you know she's leaving soon, right?"

The news slammed into Wheeler. He almost stumbled back but braced his legs and dragged in a breath. "Leaving?"

"Yeah, the big awards nomination banquet. The entire cast goes. Bellarose said I don't have to attend this but when the actual awards show takes place, I'll need you and Schmitty to watch the place."

"'Course," Schmitty said.

Wheeler stared. "How long will she be gone?"

"Half a week, by my guess."

No. He couldn't allow her to leave Washington without knowing exactly how much he wanted her. How he'd throw himself in front of a stampeding bull for her—or hell, a jet if it meant stopping her from leaving before she spoke to him.

"When does she leave?"

"Tomorrow afternoon."

"Shit. Why didn't she tell me?"

"Maybe it slipped her mind."

"I gotta head home." Wheeler turned for his truck without another word and didn't look back. Aria had told him she'd see him later, but with her schedule, later could be anytime.

That wasn't acceptable.

He was halfway to the truck before he remembered he'd left the crutch next to the ATV shed. Fuck it—he had another at home, and he'd been walking on the cast most of the day. He had to find Aria.

* * * * *

Pressing her fingertips to her lips, Aria stared out at the beauty of the land. Mountains jutted into the crystal blue sky and green valleys below were dotted with cattle. A big bird of prey swooped out of the sky and rushed the ground to catch a mouse or some other small critter. Growing up a country girl, her surroundings had always fascinated her, and now she had a deep connection to Washington.

Some of it was the beauty of the landscape, sure. But she'd be lying if she didn't admit that most of her attachment had to do with a stubborn, hard-working

193

wrangler who'd given her refuge in his barn one night.

Partnership. What the hell did that even mean? Their previous night together had been filled with passion and sweet moments tucked under the blankets, and then he'd surprised her with the gorgeous hand-tooled saddle. To a rancher's daughter, that might as well be a diamond ring.

Wheeler's eyes had glowed when he stared at her and... *told her what good partners they made?* As if they were a business transaction and not a couple.

She wrapped her arms around her middle and continued to stare over the land. From her vantage point in the small-town motel she'd stopped off at on her way to the airport, things were beautiful on the surface but feeling bleak on the inside.

She was headed back to Hollywood for a few days, but she'd left early, needing some time apart from the cast, from Wheeler.

It had become painfully clear to her that she was in much deeper than he was. At last, she'd made up her mind and taken steps toward things she wanted in her life, and look what it had gotten her.

To Wheeler, she was a warm body to comfort him at a time when he was low. She'd provided much-needed help around his place and with his animals, picking up the slack for him. And then she'd been silly enough to buy those horses and make improvements to his land.

If things were over, she had more choices to make. The horses she could move to her daddy's ranch without trouble, so it wasn't a huge deal. And what was a bit of lumber or labor costs compared to her broken heart?

Stupidly, she'd believed there might be so much more between them than a simple partnership.

Ugh. That word pissed her off.

She turned for the cheap sliding door off her motel room and went back inside. The room was simple but clean, and for that she was grateful. If she had to find a hideout, at least it didn't have bedbugs.

She flopped onto the double bed and drew her legs up to her chest. By being here, she wasn't really running again, was she? No, she'd simply taken a detour on her way to the airport, was spending time in a small town.

Call it mental recuperation before she had to return to the rat-race of an industry she didn't totally understand — and if she was honest with herself, did not love.

She rested her cheek on her knees. A tear rolled from the corner of her eye.

If I don't love it, why am I doing it?

Because it had been an opportunity nobody could turn down. Fame and money was the dream of many.

Just not Aria.

She was good at acting and it wasn't the worst job a woman could ask for. But she preferred the simple life of training horses.

Buying that pair of reining horses had given her the boost to her spirit she needed, and her hopes had sailed even high when it came to Wheeler.

How off she'd been to believe there was more between them than a partnership.

Or had she?

A man couldn't fake lovemaking like that. Wheeler had touched every inch of her with tender loving care that night... He'd stared into her eyes and watched her come apart for him with a shimmer in his eyes that had made her believe he returned her feelings.

Could it be he was really just terrible at vocalizing his true emotions?

He was a rough man, callused and work-worn. He talked to men and cattle. The softest words he probably had were for his horse. So it was completely possible that the cowboy just didn't know what to say to her.

Reading between the lines, she might hear love in his soft whispers while he was buried deep inside her or in the gleam in his eyes as he revealed the gift of the saddle.

She swallowed hard around the tears that threatened to tumble down her cheeks. She was far from perfect, was growing and learning about how to get the things she wanted in this life.

First, she wanted to end her acting stint. Horses were her true love—that and Wheeler. She was head over heels for the man, and she couldn't run from that another second. She had to go back.

Five minutes later, she was checked out of the motel and in her rental car on the way up the road again, headed toward the massive mountain range stretching along the horizon. Just beyond the foothills of those mountains was a small ranch with five very special horses on it. Not a lot, but each one important. There was a cozy house with new butcher block countertops and a porch that needed fixing.

And a cowboy with a broken foot he refused to stay off and who sucked at telling a woman how he felt about her.

Aria gripped the steering wheel and fixed her gaze on the farthest point in the road. She was going back to get her man—her decision was made.

Chapter Ten

Wheeler rolled up on King's ranch like it was on fire and he had the only bucket of water. When he jumped out of the truck, his foot gave a twinge he ignored as he ate up the ground to the enclosure where King was working with the horses.

He gave a shrill whistle, and his buddy whirled around. Concern etched on King's face as he hurried toward Wheeler.

"What's wrong?"

"Bellarose is gone?"

His brows pinched together. "Yeah, she should be at the airport by now. A bunch of the actors rode together. They fly out in an hour and a half."

"Dammit. That's what I was afraid of. Thanks!" He took off again, moving too fast to call it walking, yet he couldn't quite run on that cast, and he'd abandoned all thoughts of using the crutch.

He jumped back into his truck and took off to the road in a blaze of dust. The shocks on his truck left a lot to be desired over the humps and dips, but his mind was centered on one thing getting to Aria.

If he let her board that plane without telling her how he felt... Oh God, he could lose her. The filming wasn't yet finished for the season, so she'd have to return to the set, but once she left Washington, would she forget all about him?

He'd fucked up, pure and simple. The previous day she'd told him she'd see him later, but she'd never turned up. His biggest mistake yet had been not going after her then. But somehow, in his mind, he figured she needed some space. What an idiot he'd been to wait. If only he'd stormed the set and demanded she hear him out, he wouldn't have his heart aching in his throat right now.

He jammed his boot down on the gas pedal and sped toward the highway. The airport wasn't a long drive, but he wondered how much he could shave off if he gunned it.

As long as the flight hadn't taken off, he'd catch her. He only prayed that by some freak chance, Aria wasn't on a different flight than Bellarose.

The longer he drove, the more his mind fooled him into believing he'd lost her. He ground his molars until his head ached, but it was nothing compared to the pain in his heart. He loved the woman, wanted to spend the rest of his days with her by his side. And if he'd missed out on having the perfect woman for him because of his stupid inability to just tell her he loved her, he was going to tie himself to a horse and have it drag him behind it as punishment.

When he spotted the airport sign, his heart gave a hard leap against his chest wall. He breathed around the crash of pain and careened into the lot, found a spot and haphazardly parked.

The distance to the building made him wish he had a better mode of transportation than his damn casted foot. He'd have to make do.

He took off at a walk/run, limping as fast as he could to the big doors.

The minute he entered, he shouted at an employee. "Flight for Hollywood!"

She gave him a startled glance and then stumbled out directions to the gate. He thanked her and took off again.

Passing people sleeping in seats and parents trying to keep their offspring entertained, he hurried to the gate where the cast would board.

When he spotted Bellarose's head of thick red hair, his heart gave that crash against his ribs again. She had to be here. Aria was here.

He scanned the group of people sitting there. He didn't know much about the show — why hadn't he shown more interest in what Aria did? It was important to her, and he should have been more invested.

It was because he didn't think of her as an actor and celebrity, but just as the beautiful, tough and knowledgeable rancher who meant the universe to him.

He didn't see her among the people. Maybe she'd gone to the restroom.

"Bellarose." His voice came out like ground glass.

The woman snapped her head up, and seeing it was him, leaped to her feet. "Wheeler." Her face drained of color. "Is something wrong with King?"

"Oh God, no. I'm sorry to scare ya. I'm looking for Aria."

The blood rushed back into her face, and a hand fluttered to her chest. "Thank God. Aria... she isn't here. She left last night. She should already be in Hollywood."

The words were like bullets striking him. It was everything he'd feared, come to light. He'd waited too long, been slow to act, and now she was gone.

He tore the hat off his head and slapped it against his thigh. Everyone seated looked at him, and one guy, probably a bodyguard traveling with the actors, stood up.

Bellarose waved him back down. "It's okay. He's a friend." She grabbed Wheeler's arm and steered him a few feet off. "Did you have an argument?"

"No, I had a dumb fuck moment. Pardon my language. I wanted to tell her I love her, and it came out all wrong. She left, and I knew she wasn't happy. I should have gone after her. Fuck, why didn't I?"

She squeezed his arm. "Misunderstandings happen. It isn't the end of the world. You can still talk to her on the phone and make things right."

"What I want to say involves me getting down on one knee. Hell." He ran his hand over his face. "All right. There's nothing I can do right now. She's there and I'm here. I'll have to wait till she returns. How long will that be?"

"We resume filming on Tuesday."

Dammit. Tuesday was days away, too far off.

"Do you want me to try to text her for you?" Bellarose's eyes glowed with concern.

"No, I need to say the words myself. Thanks, though."

Just then her phone rang, and she drew it from the purse she had looped across her body. She shot Wheeler a look. "It's King."

"He's prob wondering about me showing up at Blackwater acting like a crazy person. Take the call. I'll go on home."

Bellarose gave a nod and brought the phone to her ear. As Wheeler walked away, he heard her words grow fainter and fainter.

* * * * *

Wheeler's truck wasn't in the driveway. Aria didn't think he was in town, either, as she'd just driven through there. He could be up at Blackwater working with King, but he typically went first thing in the morning when he could be of the most help with feeding and checking the herd.

Maybe he got delayed.

Aria parked the rental car and sucked in a breath of the fresh, pine-and-hay-scented air. Tears sprang to her eyes.

It shouldn't feel like she belonged here, but it did. It was as if she'd run straight for home after Jason sprang that wedding on her. Somehow, without even knowing it, she'd been led to this place that soothed her soul and had found a man who did the opposite—by stirring it.

She looked around. The place was changed with her being here.

I'm changed.

She guessed Wheeler was different as well, if the stubborn ass could admit such a thing to her. For some reason, the thought brought a touch of a smile to her lips.

When she wandered to the barn, she noted the horses were not out. Odd and somewhat disturbing. If he hadn't let them roam free for the morning, he must not plan to come back anytime soon.

What if something else had happened, an accident? It was more likely the only accident that would befall him was him taking a handsaw to his own cast.

She entered the barn. Immediately, her gaze fell over the saddle. It hadn't been moved. A pang of regret swept through her. Why hadn't she just talked it out with Wheeler at the time? She'd let her emotions run too high and only thought to escape. Well, this last time she'd learned her lesson—three times was a charm. Spending a sleepless night in that motel while longing for Wheeler had set her straight, and she would never run again. She knew her course now, and she intended to stick to it.

The horses greeted her with soft sounds, which brought a smile to her face. She drifted to Gusto's stall first. The big animal stuck his head over the door, reaching out for the carrots she typically brought him.

She patted his nose. "No treats today. I'm sorry."

He grunted.

Drifting down the line of stalls, she spoke to the mares and then the two reining horses. She knew less about them, but she intended to spend a lot of time with them the instant filming wrapped up.

If Wheeler didn't mind her working here with him, that was. But only if she set him straight. They would be much more than a partnership—she wanted it all.

After a moment of contemplation, she began to open the stall doors and lead the horses out into the fresh air. Then she leaned on the fence and watched them prance around to stretch their legs. Gusto was doing well on that leg. Maybe it wouldn't take up to nine months to heal, after all. Though he still favored it, Aria felt it was far better than some injuries she'd seen in her life.

With the horses happy, she was happy too. She cut across the yard to the house. The door was locked, a sure indication that Wheeler didn't plan to return very soon.

Pressing her lips together, she wandered back to the barn. Fatigue from her sleepless night weighed on her, pressed down on her shoulders. By the time she reached the barn, the sun on her head had done the job of warming her to a sleepy state. Her eyelids drooped.

One look at the hay bales where her saddle sat was too much for Aria. She grabbed a relatively clean blanket and tossed it over the hay, and then curled up next to her saddle. With her arm folded beneath her head, she stared at the barn door, willing her lover to come through it.

Her breaths slowed, but she didn't realize how close she was to falling asleep until her phone jolted her.

She sat up and made a grab for the device. When she saw the caller, her heart fell. "Bellarose."

"Aria. Have you heard from Wheeler?"

That had her on her feet, her boot heels scraping the barn boards. She gripped the phone tighter. "Wheeler? No. I never made it to the airport, and I turned around and came back to his place, but he isn't here."

"Oh God. He was at the airport looking for you."

A surge of joy struck her, rendering her speechless.

"Aria?" Bellarose asked.

"I'm here. You're telling me that Weheler came looking for me at the airport?"

"Yes. He seemed pretty down and out, which is why I'm calling to see if you heard from him."

She pressed her fingers to her forehead. "No," she said unevenly. "He didn't call me."

"Well, I'm sure he's on his way home now. Wait—did you say you never caught your flight out?"

"Bellarose, I won't be at the banquet. I'll call and make my apologies." It seemed she was letting down a lot of people lately, and she never seemed to be doing what was expected of her. First Jason and now this. To her thinking, it meant she was in the wrong place in her life.

"Aria, in this business, life still has to come first. Your happiness has to come first. Don't lose sight of that."

Tears burned Aria's eyes. "Thank you, Bellarose. I needed that."

"Take care. I'll see you when we get back to the set."

"Yes. Safe travels." Aria ended the call and raised her head, staring out the open barn door to the dark, empty house. Wheeler had come searching for her. She'd come back for him.

And they'd crossed paths.

She thought of getting back in her car to go looking for him, but that would be silly. He was on his way home. There was nothing to do but wait.

Returning to the hay, she lay down again with one arm slung around the gleaming saddle.

* * * * *

The sight of the small, unfamiliar car parked in Wheeler's driveway had his heart pounding out of his chest. He jumped from the truck, barely aware of the cast he shouldn't be walking on as he made his way to the barn. The door stood open.

When he reached the opening, his breath punched from his lungs.

Jesus, she's home.

Aria was fast asleep on the hay bales, curled onto her side with the saddle tucked close like a little girl who'd taken a nap on Christmas Day, tuckered out from all the excitement.

His heart throbbed into his throat, and he braced a hand on the doorframe as he watched her chest rise and fall in sleep. Her lashes, thick and lush, cast shadows across her cheeks, and her lips were plumped out, the most kissable things he'd ever seen.

Why had she come back here? She should be in Hollywood by now, and instead she'd backtracked and come full circle, falling asleep in his barn.

He was moving forward before he fully realized his intention. When he scooped his arms beneath her and gathered her close, she jerked awake.

"Wheeler!"

"Honey, you fell asleep in my barn again." Tenderness shook him to the core. God, he was in love with this woman, and he wasn't going to wait another second to tell her. "Aria—"

She was one of those women who was instantly awake and ready to take on the day, and this time was no different. She drew from his hold and climbed off the hay to stand before him. Disheveled and more beautiful than ever, she met his stare.

"I'm sorry—" he began, but she cut him off.

"Wait. I want to talk first if that's okay."

He nodded, hands fisted to keep from grabbing her and doing the talking between the sheets. Hell, he didn't want to take the time to get to the bedroom. He wanted to feel her clutching around his cock and listen to her little cries of pleasure, even if it meant having hay in places no man ever wanted it.

"Wheeler. God, it's good to see you." Her throat worked, and she raised a trembling hand to brush the warm brown hair from her eyes.

He took a step forward. "I need to touch you."

She nodded, and then she was in his arms, head tucked under his chin where it belonged. She grasped his shoulders, clinging like she never wanted to let go. Fuck, he hoped that was the case and this wasn't really a goodbye.

"Wheeler, I know you didn't mean what you were saying about the partnership. I mean, you meant it. But I don't think you want to just be partners?"

"Hell, yes, I do. But—"

She clapped a hand over his mouth. From over her fingers, he stared down at her. "I've learned a lot since I came here weeks ago and you found me asleep in your barn. I've figured things out about myself that I hadn't completely owned before, and that was how much I was letting life overtake me instead of jumping in the saddle myself. It started when I was young, I guess, and I just sort of went along with the things that were presented to me."

He stared down at her, anticipating there was more.

She dragged in a breath. "I don't want to be an actor. I'm going to ask to be written off the show."

His eyes widened, but she didn't move her hand, so he didn't speak.

"I don't love it, and life's too short to do something you don't feel completely passionate about. Those horses—I feel passionate about them. I'm going to train them up and take them to competitions, finally do what I always dreamed of."

He made a noise in his throat.

She shook her head. "I'm still talkin', mister."

His grin spread behind her hand, and her eyes shone for a brief moment before narrowing with intensity.

"As for you, cowboy, I don't just want a partner in the business. I want a partner in life. In your world.

In your bed. I'm making a big decision here, and that is you, Wheeler."

He couldn't take anymore. He grasped her wrist gently and pulled her hand away from his lips. He was too choked up to speak, yet he must tell her all the things he'd intended to a day before.

"Aria, I'm in love with you. I don't know how to be without you anymore, and I don't wanna try. I love you, and I want to spend the rest of my days with you. Marry me. Stay here on the ranch with me, and I'll build it up for you, make it everything you ever dreamed of."

A cry left her, but she was smiling. "Will you get rid of that ugly blue bathroom?"

"I'll begin demo today. Just find me a sledgehammer, honey." He wrapped her closer to his chest and butted their hips together. "Just say you'll be my wife and we can start living this very minute."

"No, we started when I woke up in that stall over there with you lookin' down at me. I love you, Wheeler." She went on tiptoe, and he swooped in at the same moment. Their lips crashed together in a seeking, emotional kiss that took long minutes to surface from.

He searched her eyes. "You're sure about quitting the show?"

She nodded. "It was a good run, but it's not for me. I'm a rancher's daughter."

"And a wrangler's fiancée?" He arched a brow in hope.

"I'm saying yes to this proposal, Wheeler. Yes, with all my heart." Her eyes flashed as she moved upward for another kiss. "And I promise I won't run."

He brushed his mouth over hers, tasting woman and the salt of her tears of joy.

Sealing the deal.

* * * * *

Watching a gorgeous and muscled man strip bare and sheath his impressive cock in a condom was every woman's wish — but being in love with the man made it so much more exciting.

Somehow, they'd made it from the barn to the bedroom, the whole process taking only minutes, yet she felt she'd lived a lifetime in those kisses and promising touches they'd shared while crossing the yard.

Aria ran her tongue over her lower lip, and Wheeler let out a growl. "Do that again, and I'll make you use that tongue."

She purposely darted her tongue along her lip again, and he tossed the condom wrapper over his shoulder. "That's it. You asked for it."

When he dived for the mattress, she opened her arms. As soon as his hard, warm body slid over hers, she began to wiggle closer. The touch of his skin against hers had her body on fire. Juices wet her inner thighs. Her need built until she couldn't hold back any longer and sought his mouth.

The kiss was a soft brushing, barely a caress. Then at the same time, they shared a sound of abandon and gave themselves up to the passion they'd been trying to stretch out.

She curled her hand around his nape, pulling him down. He swept his tongue through her mouth, sending tingles all through her. Rocking her hips upward, she showed him exactly what she wanted — now.

But he remained still, pinning her with his body, flattening her to the bed. The need snaking through her core made her hyper-aware of every flick of his tongue, every stroke of his fingertips.

His fingers teased the sensitive spot behind her jaw and down her throat, leaving a trail of white fire in their wake. He dipped one into her cleavage. Then slid it between her breasts and down around the curve of one. When he dragged it up to her taut nipple, she let out a cry.

He traced her areola in languid circles until she was arching into his touch. "Wheeler, I need your mouth on me."

Her plea went unanswered. He only continued to tease her with the roughened pad of his finger over her sensitive bud.

Two could play this game of torment. She slipped her hand between their bodies and enveloped his cock.

He went still, hazel eyes on her as if waiting to see what she'd do.

She closed her fingers into a tight ring and drew it up over the mushroomed tip of his erection.

A shudder ran through him.

"Good to know you're not immune to me," she whispered.

"Honey, I'm far from immune to you. I love you." He bent to her mouth again, his kiss wild and hungry. She matched it stroke for stroke of her tongue as she tormented him with her hand the way he was doing on her breast.

Suddenly, he broke the kiss and began to slither down her body, spattering kisses over her chest and breasts to ribs and belly. Her thighs parted for him long before he reached the place he sought, but by the time he sank his tongue between her wet folds, she was trembling.

He rumbled a growl against her pussy. His tongue anchored her in place, only the tip moving, flicking, strumming her bundle of nerves. Her pleasure level spiked, and she cried out as she gripped his shoulders. He lightened the pressure of his tongue on her clit and just as she was building toward her orgasm, he changed rhythm, keeping it just out of reach.

She dug in her short nails and let the waves of need wash over her.

With an abrupt switch, he ran his tongue down her seam and dipped it into her wetness. His warm, soft tongue barely breached her opening before he returned to her clit, circling it this time with exquisite torture. Aria bit back another cry and squeezed her eyes shut.

As she was about to begin the climb to what seemed to be the biggest orgasm of her life, he fit his fingers into her opening. Holding them there, unmoving.

He had her toeing the edge of a cliff. Then he plunged his fingers deep, and she dangled over the side of the precipice. Her insides clutched at his fingers. Her clit pulsed beneath his tongue.

A low scream left her, growing louder as waves hit her harder and harder. "Wheeler!"

Her thighs locked around his ears, and he hummed in encouragement.

She crested, peaked and let go. Her release hit with a strength that tore the cry off her lips.

* * * * *

The moment went on and on, and damn if Wheeler ever wanted his woman to stop feeling good at his hands. Each moment would not be perfect, but they'd do their best to reach those heights.

214

She bucked against his lips and tongue, and he stroked her inner wall with his fingers. A final hard contraction rocked her, and then she collapsed, gasping, fingers entangled in his hair.

"Wheeler... babe, I need you. Don't make me wait." Her brown eyes were darker with a passion that he couldn't deny another second.

Gliding up her body, he poised at the quick of her, looking down into her beautiful eyes. "Forever," he grated out.

Tears burned in her eyes. "I love you."

He cupped her jaw and kissed her at the same moment he thrust into her pussy. Liquid heat enveloped him. He had to grind his teeth against the urge to come there and then. With all the sensations coupled with his emotions for Aria, he was having a difficult time holding back.

When she began to writhe under him, he rolled with her, seating her atop him.

Her hair tumbled down over her breasts, and she offered him a sassy smile.

"Ride 'em, cowgirl." His voice was gritty from restraint.

"You're in for it, cowboy." She began to rise and fall on his cock, taking his shaft all the way to the edge of her pussy before slamming back over him. At first, her motions were timed, but soon it became apparent she was just as far gone as he was. Her breasts jiggled in his palms, her nipples straining against his thumbs as she took herself—and him—up toward a release so big, he wondered if he'd survive the fall.

Hell, he was willing to break more than his foot on this venture. And there was so much more at stake—his heart.

Looking into her deep eyes, burning with lust and love, he knew without a doubt he could trust her.

He moved his hands from her breasts around her body to her ass, helping her pump up and down on him. She threw herself forward and covered his mouth with hers. Their tongues tangled, a cry slipped loose from one of them, and then she was pulsing around him again.

The roar hit his lips before he could hold it back, and the first jet of cum shot from him. Each after that seemed to come from someplace deeper and deeper until his balls began to throb. The final blow ended on a rush of silence. His ears were ringing. Aria lay plastered to his chest, damp with perspiration and breathing heavily.

"So that's what it feels like." Her murmur against his skin took him a moment to make out.

God, he loved this woman so damn much. Nothing could be purer—not riding the trails with his horse, not the range of Blackwater nor the very mountains.

"What feels like?" His own voice was unsteady.

She twisted her head to stare up at him. One hand curled against his pec. "What it feels like to be so in love that nothing else matters in the world."

His lips quirked up at the corner. "If this is it, then I see why people toss away everything to have it."

"First thing I'm tossing away is the acting."

He smoothed a hand down her spine. "Aria, I'd never ask that of you. You can continue with the show, just live here and travel to the set, the way Bellarose does."

She smiled. "I love you for it, but I realized it isn't what I want. And I've decided that from here on, everything I choose is for myself. Or for you. We're a team now, Wheeler, whether you like it or not."

"A partnership, you'd say?"

She batted him in the shoulder. "Only if the partnership involves trusting each other enough to get rid of this box of condoms."

His heart gave a wild heave of joy. "We haven't talked about a family or anything yet."

"I'm not ready for a family, but I'm ready to have you—*only* you, with no barriers. I'm on other birth control." She shifted against him.

He moaned at the slippery feel of her body up next to his hardening cock. "Box is almost empty anyway."

"Uh-huh." She nibbled at his lips.

"Honey, if you haven't' noticed, I trusted you from the get-go."

"With your house."

"With my horse."

Her eyes gleamed as she gazed down at him. "With your heart?"

He drew her hand over his chest to the part that beat only for her. "That was yours from the get-go too."

This time when she kissed him, he felt all the love flooding into the moment. He held her fast to him. Damn if he was ever gonna let go.

Epilogue

The arena erupted with applause. Wheeler leaped to his feet, his heart wedged in his throat with total pride for his wife and all she'd accomplished this past year. The newest horse and rider to hit the National Reining Horse Association's millionaire club.

Even from here, he could see Aria's face crumple with emotion. She buried her head against her mare's side, and he saw her shoulders give a slight shake as she wept for joy.

He couldn't remain in the stands another minute. He jumped the barricade, landed on both boots and took off across the arena for her. A cheer went up as the viewers looked on at him throwing his arms around his wife and the horse both.

"Oh my God, Wheeler!"

"You did it, honey. You achieved what you set out to do, and you won!" He kissed her soundly. Applause increased, and Aria's salty tears were on his lips.

When they broke apart, she turned to the crowd and thrust a fist into the air. They went wild. Not only was she loved for her role on *Redemption Falls*, but she was admired for her choice to leave the show and follow her heart. This past year had been a dream for them both—the small wedding that took place in Montana on her family ranch.

After that, a whirlwind of a honeymoon in Texas to scout out some new stock, and for a simple wrangler like him, it was a trip of a lifetime. Finally, back to the ranch and gutting that bathroom as he'd promised her. The blue was gone, but she'd insisted on framing a bit of the wallpaper—a single goose and heart pattern—and hanging it on the wall above the door.

They'd had some setbacks in the horse training, and she hadn't believed in herself at times, but he'd pushed her to go with her gut and follow her heart.

And here she stood. The winner.

He let out a shaky breath, burning with pride and love.

After the award ceremony, and about a gazillion photos of both of them and many with the mare as well, Aria turned to him.

"Wheeler. Thank you."

He straightened. "What are you thanking me for? You did all of it. These past two years felt like a blink of time to me, but you busted your butt."

She shook her head. Tears began to fall. "Thank you for taking me in, then showing me that I needed to change my life in order to find the happiness I craved in the things I love."

Sliding an arm around her back, he pulled her close. Their hats bumped as they drew together. Her eyes were shiny, and happiness etched all over her beautiful face. "Aria, it's me who should be thanking you for tossing me out of my boring life and giving me so much more."

She caught his hand. Turning his palm downward, she pressed it to her stomach, low.

"Wheeler..."

It took him less than two heartbeats to understand what she was telling him. She'd gone off her birth control. And now they were going to embark on the next journey of their life together.

A choked cry left him. He snatched her up into his arms and whirled her, his mouth on hers as they shared a gleeful laugh.

"You're happy then?"

He set her down gently. "Happy? Holy hell, woman, if I don't burst and explode all over this arena, it will be a shock. I love you so damn much, and there's already a spot in my heart for this little bean growing inside you." He covered her stomach again with his hand.

She rested hers atop his. "We're both in for a ride."

"With you, I'm ready for anything, honey." He leaned in for another kiss.

THE END

EM PETROVA
WWW.EMPETROVA.COM

Em Petrova

Em Petrova was raised by hippies in the wilds of Pennsylvania but told her parents at the age of four she wanted to be a gypsy when she grew up. She has a soft spot for babies, puppies and 90s Grunge music and believes in Bigfoot and aliens. She started writing at the age of twelve and prides herself on making her characters larger than life and her sex scenes hotter than hot.

She burst into the world of publishing in 2010 after having five beautiful bambinos and figuring they were old enough to get their own snacks while she pounds away at the keys. In her not-so-spare time, she is fur-mommy to a Labradoodle named Daisy Hasselhoff.

Find Em Petrova at empetrova.com

Other Indie Titles by Em Petrova
Knight Ops Series
ALL KNIGHTER
HEAT OF THE KNIGHT
HOT LOUISIANA KNIGHT
AFTER MIDKNIGHT

KNIGHT SHIFT
O' CHRISTMAS KNIGHT
ANGEL OF THE KNIGHT

6-Pack Cowboys Series
6-PACK RANCHER
6-PACK WRANGLER

Wild West Series
SOMETHING ABOUT A LAWMAN
SOMETHING ABOUT A SHERIFF
SOMETHING ABOUT A BOUNTY HUNTER
SOMETHING ABOUT A MOUNTAIN MAN

Operation Cowboy Series
KICKIN' UP DUST
SPURS & SURRENDER

The Boot Knockers Ranch Series
PUSHIN' BUTTONS
BODY LANGUAGE
REINING MEN
ROPIN' HEARTS

ROPE BURN
COWBOY NOT INCLUDED
CUPID COWBOYS

The Boot Knockers Ranch Montana
COWBOY BY CANDLELIGHT
THE BOOT KNOCKER'S BABY
ROPIN' A ROMEO

Country Fever Series
HARD RIDIN'
LIP LOCK
UNBROKEN
SOMETHIN' DIRTY

Rope 'n Ride Series
BUCK
RYDER
RIDGE
WEST
LANE
WYNONNA

FEVERED HEARTS
WRONG SIDE OF LOVE

Club Ties Series
LOVE TIES
HEART TIES
MARKED AS HIS
SOUL TIES
ACE'S WILD

Firehouse 5 Series
ONE FIERY NIGHT
CONTROLLED BURN
SMOLDERING HEARTS

The Quick and the Hot Series
DALLAS NIGHTS
SLICK RIDER
SPURRED ON

READ ON for a sneak peek of KICKIN'
UP DUST, book 1 of the Operation Cowboy
Series...

Chapter One

"First thing I'm going to do is hug my momma and ask if she's made any biscuits." Brodie rubbed a hand over his stomach, sliding his Marine Corps T-shirt over his hard abs. "My gut's been growling for three tours."

In his early years as a Marine, he'd dreamt of Momma's light, fluffy biscuits going down with homemade peach jam. It was one of the only things from his past that hadn't faded. He couldn't quite remember how his momma's face looked, but he did recall the stern lines between his father's brows. He'd seen those twin creases enough growing up. They were etched into his brain.

"I haven't been dreaming about biscuits for three tours," Wydell drawled.

"He's been dreamin' about your momma," Garrett quipped.

"You should hear how loud he is," Boyd added.

The laughter of his three childhood buddies filled the car. They'd crawled alongside him in the desert sands of Afghanistan, and then through two more tours in Iraq. But the car had a hole where Matt would have sat.

While they fired off more jokes about who was noisiest in his bunk, Brodie stared at the gray ribbon of road stretching ahead. All four windows of the old Ford were rolled down, and he dragged in a huge breath of Texas air. Home was near. He could smell it.

Garrett, in shotgun, nudged Brodie with his elbow. "The old Ford's gotten us here."

"Yeah, she's done well." Brodie swiped his fingers through the dust on the dashboard. The plastic was cracked after being baked in the Texas sun for the past eighteen years. Yeah, she was nothing to look at but would get them to the end of the line — Los Vista, Texas. And on their pooled budget of $998.

As astute as always, Garrett picked up on Brodie's mood. Brodie forced a smile. He felt his eyes crinkle with it, but his chest was devoid of happiness. "I don't know why they're talking about my momma. It's yours we all dreamed of as teens."

Garrett groaned. "God, don't talk about my mother."

Brodie laughed, this time for real. They'd all discussed Mrs. Gentry's toned figure enough times to know Garrett didn't appreciate it. Eventually he'd taken to tackling whoever mentioned her tits.

Brodie's amusement faded as they passed a road sign for a town just outside of Los Vista. His homecoming was darkened by what he was bringing back with him—the belongings of one Sergeant Matt Pope. Best friend, platoon leader.

The familiar knot clogged Brodie's throat at the thought of all the townsfolk who'd waved them off with a parade years ago. He'd only returned as often as he could in the first year or two, but Matt had come more often to see his family between tours of duty.

Now Matt wouldn't come back at all, and Brodie was the most logical person to deliver the folded flag and dog tags to his family.

"Damn," he murmured, but nobody heard. The wind carried his curse away, though the whole car seemed to take on Brodie's state of mind. In the back, the guys settled. Garrett looked out his window.

Even the enormous Texas sky seemed too low right then. It didn't leave Brodie a lot of breathing room, and his chest started to burn.

He counted to fifty. Then backward. By fives and tens. His method of dealing with panic attacks hardly worked, but at least it distracted him for the last twenty miles of their drive.

By the time they reached the county line, his anxiety transformed to a lurch of excitement. *Home.* Miles of fields dotted with cattle. The familiar gates of the ranch that had been in his family for two generations.

Garrett leaned forward and moved his face closer to the windshield. "Where the hell is it? We shoulda been passing DeLoe's Farm Supply by now."

Brodie swung his head left and right, searching for landmarks, but the sides of the road were empty, save for some paved lots.

Then he saw it—a wooden structure caved in on itself. He blinked as he drove past, and the guys stretched their necks to see too.

"What the fuck was that?" Brodie asked.

"I think it was...Marley's Insurance office?"

"Nah, couldn't be. It's up the road a ways." Brodie strained to see farther ahead. Strange how the road was empty too. They hadn't passed a single car coming out of Los Vista. Their hometown wasn't exactly big, but it was always busy. There wasn't a lazy or idle person in Los Vista.

"No, man, I saw the sign," Garrett said.

Brodie threw a look in the side mirror but couldn't make out what Garrett meant. All he saw was a heap of fallen wood.

Realization slammed him smack in the forehead. The place was just...gone. "Holy. Fuck." The words came out of Brodie like a prayer—a prayer for him to be hallucinating. Surely what he was seeing wasn't real.

Their town—leveled. The school a jumble of bricks and glass. Cars twisted and upside down. Trees snapped off like toothpicks. The few restaurants in ruins.

Beyond that, nothing. He couldn't see a barn or silo for miles.

"Jesus Christ, what happened?" he breathed. He'd been in range of a couple grenade blasts during his time as a Marine, and the concussions had rattled him though they had done no damage. He felt the same way now—as if he'd been thrown by a blast.

"It's fucking gone. The town's gone. Either there was a war here or a tornado."

"But...nobody said anything to me. My parents didn't say anything about a tornado," Garrett said.

Brodie slowed the car and stopped in the middle of the road. There was no risk—they were totally alone.

For long seconds, nobody spoke. He had a crawling sensation that he was back in combat, looking at the devastation their team had wrought. But no, this was definitely natural. The trees weren't lopped off from bombs. They were snapped and twisted from high winds.

"Where the fuck's my barn?" Garrett's voice raised as he thrust a finger toward the place his ranch should be in the distance. "It should be there."

Brodie exchanged a glance with him and then stomped on the gas. As they thundered up the road at eighty miles an hour, he had a distinct feeling of being in an apocalypse movie. The wild birds of panic flapped in his chest again, but no amount of counting would distract him this time.

* * * * *

"Garrett's family's living in a lean-to on their property. Their cattle are all gone with the rest of the ranch." Brodie's father eyed him from the head of the table. Between them were roast beef, mashed potatoes, corn, and those light, fluffy biscuits he'd been dreaming of.

But now they were untouched.

Brodie shook his head. "How'd the tornado miss us?"

His momma lifted a shoulder in a depressed shrug. Guilt reflected in her deep brown eyes. Their four walls were still standing, if a little battered. They hadn't lost many head of cattle, while their neighbors and friends had lost everything. Momma had survivor's guilt.

Boy, did he know all about that.

"The only other property that didn't take a big hit is the Pope Ranch."

Brodie's head snapped up at his father's words. Suddenly, there was no way he could eat those biscuits or anything else on the table.

He felt himself nod. "That's good. They've...lost enough."

Of course the family had been informed of Matt's death. They hadn't traveled to Arlington Cemetery to see him buried, which was how Brodie came to possess the flag that had covered his coffin. The coffin he and his buddies had carried.

He shook himself and snagged a biscuit. The sooner he visited the Popes, the better. Then he could let his past go, stop being a Marine and start being a cowboy. They all shared this dream, but it looked as though his friends would have a harder time, seeing how they no longer had ranches.

"And the people just lost heart," Momma said, pushing the crock of jam in his direction.

"They left?"

"Almost all moved to surrounding towns."

"But the ranches...their land. How can they just leave it?"

"Many are taking insurance payouts and putting their acreage up for sale. Rebuilding is a huge undertaking. Many aren't up to the challenge. The Popes still have their place, though." His pa forked potatoes into his mouth.

What a fucked-up mess. Coming home to find they didn't have a town? And only Brodie had a home—the other guys were camping out in Garrett's family lean-to.

"How much cattle you running?" Brodie looked at his father. Now that he was back, he realized his memories of his pa's face weren't really perfect. Either that or his father had changed. Aged.

Hell, I have too. What were his parents seeing on his face? Lines from squinting into a scope all day, waiting to snipe some general before their whole platoon was killed. Brodie's skin had been tanned to leather, and he bore a jagged scar down the side of his face.

But all these changes might have taken place if he'd stayed in Los Vista and cowboy'd. The lines and tan naturally occurring from the sun, the scar from being kicked by a bull. It happened.

"Just a hundred." His father said the word like *hunnerd*.

Brodie gaped. A hundred head of cattle? Back in the day, they ran triple that. "I guess that means you don't have any ranch hands."

"Nope. And the bulls? Gone. I had them separated in the west pasture when the storm came through."

Shhhit. No bulls? What kind of ranch survived without bulls? And why hadn't Pa bought more at auction?

"Times have changed, son. The money's stretched so thin we can't rescue the ranch. We're clinging on here. Don't rightly know for how long."

Brodie set his fork and knife down with a clatter and stared between his parents. "Are you thinking about pulling out too?"

Momma reached across the table and rested a hand on his forearm. The touch felt foreign as hell—when was the last time he'd had a woman's touch, even his mother's?

"It's hard, honey. We never realized how much support we had from the neighbors. And your pa and

I aren't getting any younger. We can't use what little savings we have to buy more cattle."

"What about calves? It's time to breed so we have calves." Brodie's appetite was gone, even though he stared longingly at his plate. The home-cooked meal should have topped off a wonderful homecoming. But he still had to visit the Popes.

His father polished off a biscuit. "I don't see us having any calves, Brodie."

"Shit." He pushed away from the table.

"Brodie, where are you going?" His mother's voice pitched higher as he strode from the kitchen.

"Over to the Popes'. I'll be back by dark." He grabbed the paper bag and headed out on foot. Garrett and the other guys had the car because Boyd and Wydell had tracked down their parents to the neighboring town. Tomorrow they'd drive over and have their reunion. Brodie didn't mind walking. Besides, the Popes' place bordered theirs.

Tall grasses swished against his legs as he crossed the field. It was high time to make hay. Why hadn't his pa cut it at least? And surely there was a guy or two left in Los Vista to hire for a couple days' work.

As he crested the hill and set eyes on the Popes' ranch house, a knife of regret sliced through his chest. He issued a ragged breath and fought the memory of Matt's final moments. Cradled in Brodie's arms, blood trickling from his mouth.

Take care of yourself, Pup. Those were his last words before his eyes had glazed over and he'd stared sightlessly at the sky. The wrong sky—not a Texas sky.

They were all supposed to grow old together, get together once a week for poker games and to shoot the shit. But Matt had bugged out early, and now it was up to Brodie to hold the group together.

Only they couldn't possibly all stay in Los Vista. Not without a miracle.

A dog barked, and he searched the land for a glimpse of the animal. When he saw the black hound bounce above the grasses, ears flopping, Brodie's heart lurched. His eyes blurred as a total sense of joy overcame him.

The dog rushed him. Hit him square in the chest with his enormous paws, rocking Brodie back. He laughed and hooked the dog around the neck. "Hey, Crow. How are ya, boy?"

Crow wagged not only his tail but his whole body. He snaked his pink tongue out and licked Brodie's nose.

It had been Matt's idea to name the stray puppy Crow, partly because of its coloring and partly because they'd found him near the ruins. On the outskirts of town, a cave was hidden in the land, but most of the residents of Los Vista knew about it and had visited it at some point. The guys had taken plenty of girls there, knowing they'd be spooked enough to want the boys' arms around them.

Nobody knew what Indian tribe had inhabited the cave, but there were plenty of drawings and some artifacts. The dog had been found near enough the cave that Matt had called it an Indian pup, and it had become Old Crow. Just Crow for short.

He patted the dog on the back and it dropped to all fours. Together they walked the rest of the way to the long ranch house. Each step felt weightier. Crow stopped wagging his tail and paced slowly alongside him.

The house was unchanged, bar a few shingles that had been torn off the roof during the storm. Of course, the miles of fence running between properties was ripped up or the posts were slanted.

Brodie stepped onto the low, wooden porch. Here they'd played cowboys and Indians as boys. They'd sat on the steps and had their first stolen sips of beer.

When he pulled open the screen door, it still gave a pleasant creak. He rapped on the familiar wood while Crow panted at his side. He tried not to think of his reason for being there or what he was going to say. There were no words for this occasion. He'd do what he'd always done in times like this—he'd wing it.

Footsteps sounded inside, and his heart began to race. The throb spread until his temples ached and his eyeballs felt as if they were bulging.

Fifty, forty-nine, forty-eight...

The door opened, and he found himself staring at slim bare feet with red painted toenails. He followed them up to narrow ankles, curvy calves, thighs the warm, smooth color of a brown egg. He let his gaze rush the rest of the way up to the woman's face.

His jaw dropped.

Her full, ripe lips fell open.

For a heartbeat, he couldn't think of who this gorgeous, tawny creature was. Long, dark hair that spilled over rounded breasts. Her eyes the same color as —

"Pup!" She launched herself at Brodie, climbing him like a tree.

On reflex, he locked his arms around her and held her to him, his panic forgotten, a low ache spinning through his gut. His cock twitched at the feel of her crotch against his fly, warm and covered only by a thin strip of denim and some cotton panties. At least that's what fantasy played in his head.

"Danica?" he choked out, catching a whiff of her hair that left him with a strangely familiar feeling. She smelled of hayfields and bonfires. Of sour apples and everything he'd loved about spending time with the Popes.

"Jesus Christ, Brodie. Oh dear God." She wrapped her arms and legs around him, unwilling to let go.

He held her effortlessly, though Matt's kid sister was nearly as tall as he was. Flat-footed she must have reached six feet. "Holy fuck, Danica." He buried his face against her hair and just breathed. If driving into Los Vista had left him feeling empty, holding Danica felt like coming home.

She pulled back to look into his eyes. The cornflower depths of hers were filled with tears, and while her smile was wide and her teeth blindingly white, he saw the glint of pain in her eyes.

Very gently, he set her on her feet. She stood before him, tall and curvy. A real cowgirl in a plaid top rolled to the elbows and knotted at the waist, affording him a glimpse of tanned midriff.

Fucking hell, she wore a silver hoop in her bellybutton.

He snapped his gaze back to her face in time to see her features crumple.

"Oh sweetie." He reeled her into his arms again, just holding her and swaying back and forth as her grief crowded out the feelings of happiness they'd shared. The bag he still held seemed to weigh a hundred pounds, and he kept his wrist cocked so the bag didn't touch her back. He wasn't ready for her to ask what was inside. Right now, he just wanted to hold her.

"When did you get in?" she sniffled.

"Few hours ago."

"And…" Her breath washed over his neck, raising hairs he didn't realize he had there.

"And the town's a fucking mess."

"Nobody told you?"

He shook his head. When she withdrew from his hold to meet his stare, she'd composed herself a little. No tears wet her cheeks though some lingered in her eyes. She waved at the porch furniture, and he nodded.

Her tanned bare feet made scuffing noises as she crossed the porch, and she tucked them under her as she sat in an old wooden chair with a cushion. Brodie purposely skirted a certain chair and sank into another. One that didn't hold so many memories of the man — or boy, rather — who used to sit there.

Brodie's throat clogged again. He set the bag on the floor between his feet, leaned his elbows on his knees, and dropped his head into his hands. *Forty-seven, forty-six, forty-five.*

A whispery touch on his arm made him look up into those tear-bright eyes that were breaking his goddamn heart. "I'm glad you're home, Pup. It's good to see you."

He reached for the bag, but she tightened her grip on his arm. Her fingers were long and slender, shaped so much like her brother's.

"I know what you brought, but I'm not ready to see it, okay? Let's just talk. Like old times. Please?"

He bobbed his head in agreement and sat back in his chair to look at the only thing left in Los Vista worth seeing. Matt's kid sister had certainly grown up.

BUY YOUR COPY ON AMAZON

Made in the USA
Middletown, DE
13 June 2023

32502209R00139